I0778399

Charles E. Van Loan

Old Man Curry

Outlook

Charles E. Van Loan

Old Man Curry

1. Auflage | ISBN: 978-3-73262-312-9

Erscheinungsort: Frankfurt am Main, Deutschland

Erscheinungsjahr: 2018

Outlook Verlag GmbH, Frankfurt.

Charles E. Van Loan

Old Man Curry

Outlook

THE BOOKS OF
CHARLES E. VAN LOAN
Memorial Edition

OLD MAN CURRY
STORIES OF THE RACE TRACK

OLD MAN CURRY
RACE TRACK STORIES

BY
CHARLES E. VAN LOAN

NEW YORK
GEORGE H. DORAN COMPANY
MCMXIX

My Dear "Purdue" McCormick:—

It is customary to dedicate a book, the author selecting a good natured person to stand sponsor for his work. There are 100,000,000 people in this country, and I have selected you as Old Man Curry's godfather. When you reflect upon this statistical statement, the size of the compliment should impress you.

Then too, you love a good horse—I have often heard you say so. You love a good horse in spite of the fact that you once harnessed Colonel Jack Chinn's thoroughbred saddle animal to a trap, the subsequent events producing a better story than any you will find in these pages. Nevertheless, my dear sir, they are respectfully, even firmly dedicated to you.

Yours very sincerely,
Charles E.
Van Loan

To E. O. McCormick,
San Francisco, Cal.

———————————

OLD MAN CURRY

LEVELLING WITH ELISHA

The Bald-faced Kid shivered as he roosted on the paddock fence, for the dawn was raw and cold and his overcoat was hanging in the back room of a pawnbroker's establishment some two hundred miles away. Circumstances which he had unsuccessfully endeavoured to control made it a question of the overcoat or the old-fashioned silver stop watch. The choice was not a difficult one. "I can get along without the benny," reflected the Kid, "because I'm naturally warm-blooded, but take away my old white kettle and I'm a soldier gone to war without his gun."

In the language of the tack rooms, the Bald-faced Kid was a hustler—a free lance of the turf, playing a lone hand against owner and bookmaker, matching his wits against secret combinations and operating upon the wheedled capital of the credulous. He was sometimes called a tout, but this he resented bitterly, explaining the difference between a tout and a hustler. "A tout will have six suckers betting on six different horses in the same race. Five of 'em have to lose. A tout is guessing all the time, but a hustler is likely to know something. One horse a race is my motto—sometimes only one horse a day, but I've got to know something before I lead the sucker into the betting ring…. What is a sucker? Huh! He's a foolish party who bets money for a wise boy because the wise boy never has any money to bet for himself!"

Picking winners was the serious business of the Kid's life, hence the early morning hours and the careful scrutiny of the daybreak workouts.

Bitter experience had taught the Kid the error of trusting men, but up to a certain point he trusted horses. He depended upon his silver stop watch to divide the thoroughbreds into two classes—those which were short of work and those which were ready. The former he eliminated as unfit; the latter he ceased to trust, for the horse which is ready becomes a betting tool, at the mercy of the bookmaker, the owner, and the strong-armed little jockey.

"Which one are they going to bet on to-day?" was the Kid's eternal question. "Which one is going to carry the checks?"

Across the track, dim in the gray light, a horse broke swiftly from a canter into the full racing stride. Something clicked in the Kid's palm.

"Got you!" he muttered.

His eye followed the horse up the back stretch into the gloom of the upper turn where the flying figure was lost in the deep shade of the trees. One shadow detached itself from the others and appeared at the head of the straightaway. The muffled thud of hoofs became audible, rising in swift crescendo as the shadow resolved itself into a gaunt bay horse with a tiny negro boy crouched motionless in the saddle. A rush, a flurry, a spatter of clods, a low-flying drift of yellow dust and the vision passed, but the Bald- faced Kid had seen enough to compensate him for the early hours and the lack of breakfast. He glanced at his watch.

"Old Elisha, under wraps and fighting for his head," was his comment. "The nigger didn't let him out any part of the way…. Oh, you prophet of Israel!"

"What did that bird step the three-quarters in?" asked a voice, and the Kid turned to confront Squeaking Henry, also a hustler, and at times a competitor.

"Dunno; I didn't clock him," lied the Kid.

"That was Old Man Curry's nigger Mose," continued Squeaking Henry, so-called because of his plaintive whine, "and I was wondering if the horse wasn't Elijah. I didn't get a good look at him. Maybe it was Obadiah or Nehemiah. Did you ever hear such a lot of names in your life? They tell me Old Man Curry got 'em all out of the Bible." The Kid nodded. "Bible horses are in fine company at this track," chuckled Squeaking Henry. "I been here a week now, and darned if I can get onto the angles. I guess Old Man Curry is the only owner here who ain't doin' business with some bookmaker or other. Look at that King William bird yesterday! He was twenty pounds the best in the race and he come fifth. The jock did everything to him but cut his throat. What are you goin' to do when they run 'em in and out like that?… Say, Kid, was that Elijah or was it another one of them Bible beetles? I didn't get a good look at him."

The Bald-faced Kid stole a sidelong glance at Squeaking Henry.

"Neither did I," said he. "Why don't you ask Old Man Curry which horse it was? He'd tell you. He's just foolish enough to do it."

Halfway up the back stretch a shabby, elderly man leaned against a fence, thoughtfully chewing a straw as he watched the little negro check the bay horse to a walk. He had the flowing beard of a patriarch, the mild eye of a deacon, the calm, untroubled brow of a philosopher, and his rusty black frock coat lent him a certain simple dignity quite rare upon the race tracks of the Jungle Circuit. In the tail pocket of the coat was something rarer still—a well- thumbed Bible, for this was Old Man Curry, famous as the owner of Isaiah, Elijah, Obadiah, Esther, Ezekiel, Jeremiah, Elisha, Nehemiah, and Ruth. In his spare moments he read the Psalms of David for pleasure in their rolling cadences and the Proverbs of Solomon for profit in their wisdom, which habit alone was sufficient to earn for him a reputation for eccentricity.

Old Man Curry clinched this general opinion by entering into no entangling alliances with brother owners, and the bookmaker did not live who could call him friend. He attended strictly to his own business, which was training horses and racing them to win, and while he did not swear, drink liquor, or smoke, he proved he was no Puritan by chewing fine-cut tobacco and betting on his horses when he thought they had a chance to win and the odds were to his liking. For the latter he claimed Scriptural precedent.

"Wasn't the children of Israel commanded to spile the Egyptians?" said he. "Wasn't they? Well, then! the way I figger it times has changed a lot since then, but the principle's the same. There's some children of Israel making book 'round here that need to be spiled a heap worse'n Pharaoh ever did." Then, after thought: "But you got to go some to spile bad eggs." As the little negro drew near, the blackness of his visage was illuminated by a sudden flash of ivory. Elisha snorted and shook his head from side to side. Old Man Curry stepped forward and laid his hand upon the bridle.

"Well, Mose?" said he. The small rider gurgled as he slipped from the saddle:

"Nothin' to it, nothin' to it a-a-atall. 'Is 'Lisha bird, he's ready to fly. Yes, suh, he's prepaihed to show all 'em otheh hawsses which way 'is track runs!"

"Went good, did he, Mose?"

"Good! He like to pull my ahms off, 'at's how good he went! Yes, suh, he was jus' buck-jumpin' all 'e way down 'at stretch. 'Ey kin all be in front of him tuhnin' fo' to-morreh, an' he'll go by 'em so fas' 'ey won't know which way he went!"

Old Man Curry nodded. "Elisha ain't no front runner," said he. "He's like his daddy—does all his running in the last quarter. He comes from behind."

"Sure does!" chirped Mose. "All I got to do is fetch him into 'e stretch, swing wide so he got plenty of room to ambulate hisse'f, boot him once in 'e slats, an'—good night *an'* good-by! Ol 'Lisha jus' tip his to 'em otheh hawsses an' say: "Scuse me, gen'elmen an' ladies, but I got mos' uhgent business down yondeh 'bout quahteh of a mile; 'em judges waitin' faw me.' 'At's what he say, boss. Nothin' to it a-a-atall."

"Give him plenty of room, Mose."

"Sutny will. Won't git me nothin' stickin' on 'at rail. 'Em white bu'glahs don't seem to crave me nohow, no time; 'ey jus' be tickled to death to put me an' 'Lisha oveh 'e fence if we git clost 'nough to it. Yes, indeed; I 'low to give 'is hawss all 'e room whut is on a race track!"

Old Man Curry led Elisha toward his barn, the little negro trailing behind, addressing the horse in terms of endearment. "You ol' wolf, on'iest way to beat you to-morreh is to saw all yo' laigs off. You as full of run as a hydrant, 'at's whut you are, ain't you, 'Lisha?"

Two horsemen were standing in the door of a feed room as the queer procession passed. They interrupted a low-toned conversation to exchange significant glances. "Speak of the devil," said one, "and there he goes now. Been working that horse for the last race to-morrow."

"It won't get him anything," said the other. "You can forget that he's entered."

The first speaker was short and stout, with no personal beauty to be marred by the knife scar which ran from the lobe of his left ear to the point of his chin, a broad, red welt in the blackish stubble of his beard. This was Martin O'Connor, owner of the Sunrise racing stable, sometimes know as Grouchy O'Connor.

His companion was a smooth-faced, dapper, gold-toothed blond, apparently not more than twenty-five years of age. Innocence circled his sleek towhead like a halo; good cheer radiated from him in ceaseless waves. His glance was direct and compelling and his smile invited confidences; he seemed almost too young and entirely too artless for his surroundings. The average observer would have pitied him for a lamb among wolves, and the pity would have been misplaced, for Al Engle was older than he looked by several sinful semesters and infinitely wiser than he had any honest right to be. His frank, boyish countenance was at once a cloak and an asset; it had beguiled many a man to his financial hurt. He was shrewd, intelligent, unscrupulous, and acquisitive; the dangerous head of a small clique of horse owners which was doing its bad best to remove the element of chance from the sport of kings. In his touting days he had been given the name of the Sharpshooter and in his prosperity it clung to him.

"Forget that he's entered, eh?" repeated O'Connor. "Elisha—Elisha—I don't seem to place that horse."

"His name used to be Silver Star," said the Sharpshooter.

"That dog?" said O'Connor, disgustedly. "Let's see; wasn't he at Butte last season?"

"Yes. Cricket Caley owned him."

"The little old jock that died last spring?"

"Same one. This horse Silver Star was all he had and Cricket used to ride him himself. Rank quitter. I've seen Caley boot and kick and slash this bird until he wore himself out; he'd quit just the same. Wouldn't run a lick after he got into the stretch.

"Then one day Cricket slipped him over at a long price. Don't know how he did it. Hop, most likely. Got somebody to bet on Silver Star at 25 to 1 and took quite a little chunk of money out of the ring. That was Caley's last race; he'd been cheating the undertakers for years. Before he died he gave the horse to Old Man Curry. They'd been friends, but if a friend of mine gave me a horse like that and didn't throw in a dog collar, he couldn't run fast enough to get away from me. Curry put in an application to the Jockey Club and had the name changed from Silver Star to Elisha. Won't have anything but Bible names, the old nut!

"Curry hasn't won with him yet, and I'd hate to be hanging by the neck until he does, because if ever there was a no-account hound masquerading with a mane and tail, it's the one you just saw go by here. He won't gather anything to-morrow. Forget him."

O'Connor hesitated a moment; he was a cautious soul. "Might tell Grogan and Merritt to look after him," he suggested.

"No need to. And that bullet-headed little nigger wouldn't like anything better than a chance to holler to the judges. The horse ain't got a chance, I tell you. Wouldn't have with the best rider in the world. Forget him."

"Well—just as you say, Al. Broadsword's good enough to beat him, I reckon."

"Of course he is! Forget this Elisha. Go on and figure just the same as if he wasn't in the race."

The Sharpshooter and his friends, through their betting commissioners, backed Broadsword from 4 to 1 to even money. The horse was owned by O'Connor and ridden by Jockey Grogan. Bald Eagle, Amphion, and Remorseful were supposed to be the contenders, but their riders jogged blithely to the post with Broadsword tickets in their bootlegs and riding orders of a sort to make those pasteboards valuable.

Jockey Moseby Jones, on Elisha, was overlooked when these favours were surreptitiously distributed, but his bootleg was not empty. There was a ticket in it which called for twenty-two dollars in case Elisha won—a two-dollar bet at 10 to 1. It was put there by Old Man Curry just before the bugle blew.

"Bring him home in front, Mose," said the old man.

"Sutny will!" grinned the negro. "You betting much on him, boss?"

"I visited a while with the children of Israel," said Curry gravely. "Remember now—lots of room when you turn for home."

"Yes, suh. I won't git clost 'nough to 'em scound'els faw 'em do nothin' but say 'Heah he comes' an' 'Yondeh he goes.' Won't slam me into no fence; I'm comin' back by ovehland route!"

Later O'Connor, who had been bidden to forget Elisha, remembered him. Broadsword led into the stretch by four open lengths, hugging the rail. Mose trailed the bunch around the upper turn, brought Elisha smartly to the outside, kicked the bay horse in the ribs with his spurs and said:

"Whut yo' doin' heah? Go 'long about yo' business!"

Jockey Grogan, already spending his fifty-dollar ticket, heard warning yells from the rear and sat down to ride, but it was too late. Elisha, coming with a tremendous rush, was already on even terms with Broadsword. Three strides and daylight showed between them. It was all over but the shouting, and there was very little of that, for Elisha had few friends in the crowd.

"Hah!" ejaculated the presiding judge, tugging at his stubby grey moustache. "Old Man Curry put one over on the boys, or I miss my guess. Yes, sir, he beat the good thing and spilled the beans. Elisha, first; Broadsword, second; that thing of Engle's, third. Serves 'em right! Hah!"

Martin O'Connor standing on the outskirts of the betting ring, searching a limited vocabulary for language with which to garnish his emotions, felt a nudge at his elbow. It was the Sharpshooter.

"Go away from me! Don't talk to me!" sputtered O'Connor. "You make me sick! I thought you said that dog couldn't run! You're a swell prophet, you are, you—you——"

Al Engle smiled as he slipped his binoculars into the case. "I may not be a prophet," said he, "but I'll have one in my barn to-night."

"Huh?"

"Oh, nothing, only that's too good a horse for Curry to own. I'm going to take Elisha away from him."

"Going to run him up?"

"As far as the old man will go."

"Well, look out you don't start a selling-race war."

The Sharpshooter sneered. "Curry hasn't got nerve enough to fight us," said he.

Now the "selling race" is an institution devised and created for the protection of owners against owners, the theory being to prevent the running of horses out of their proper class.

An owner, entering a selling race, must set a price upon his horse—let us say five hundred dollars. Should the horse win, it must be offered for sale at that figure, the owner being given the right to protect his property in a bidding contest.

In case the animal changes hands, the original owner receives five hundred dollars, and no more. If the horse has been bid up to one thousand dollars, the racing association shares the run-up with the owner of the horse which finished second. It will readily be seen that this system discourages the practice of entering a two-thousand-dollar horse in a five-hundred-dollar selling race, but it also permits a disgruntled owner to revenge himself upon a rival. Some of the bitterest feuds in turf history have grown out of "selling- race wars."

Little Mose brought Elisha back into the ring, saluted the judges, and, dismounting, began to unsaddle. Old Man Curry came wandering down the track from the paddock gate where he had watched the race. He was chewing a straw reflectively, and the tails of his rusty black frock coat flapped in the breeze like the garment of a scarecrow. Mose, with the saddle, bridle, blanket, and weight pad in his arms, disappeared under the judges' stand where the clerk of the scales weighed him together with his tackle.

The associate judge came out on the steps of the pagoda with a programme in his hand. Mose bounced into view, handed his tackle to Shanghai, Curry's hostler, and started for the jockeys' room, singing to himself out of sheer lightness of heart. He knew what he would do with that twenty-two-dollar ticket. There was a crap game every night at the O'Connor stable.

"All right, judge!" called the clerk of the scales. "Shoot!"

The associate judge cleared his throat, nodded to Old Man Curry, fingered his programme, and began to speak in a dull, slurring monotone, droning out the formula as prescribed for such occasions:

"Elisha—winner'v this race—entered to be sold—four hundred dollars—— Any bids?"

"Five hundred!"

Old Man Curry, leaning against the top rail of the fence, started slightly and turned his eyes in the direction of the sound. The Sharpshooter flashed his gold teeth at him in a cheerful smile. Old Man Curry shrugged his shoulders and rolled the straw from one corner of his mouth to the other. The associate judge looked at him, asking a question with his eyebrows. There was a stir in the crowd about the stand. A bidding contest is always an added attraction.

"Friend, you don't want this hoss," expostulated Old Man Curry, addressing

Engle. "He ain't a race hoss; he's a *trick* hoss. You don't want him."

"What about you, Curry?" asked the associate judge.

"Oh, well," said the old man, slowly. "*And* five."

"Six hundred!"

Old Man Curry seemed annoyed. He combed his beard with his fingers.

"*And* five," said he.

"Seven hundred!"

Old Man Curry took time for reflection. Then he sighed deeply.

"Maybe you want him worse'n I do, friend," said he. "*And* five."

"Eight hundred!"

Old Man Curry smothered an impatient ejaculation, threw away his straw and ransacked his pockets for his packet of fine-cut.

"Might as well make it a good one while we're at it," said he. "*And* five."

"One thousand!" said the Sharpshooter, his smile broadening. "Pretty fair price for a trick horse, eh, Curry?"

The old man paused with a generous helping of tobacco halfway to its destination. He regarded Engle with unblinking gravity.

"'The words of his mouth were smoother than butter,' he quoted, 'but war was in his heart.' That's from Psalms, young man…. Now, it's this way with a trick hoss: a lot depends on whether you know the trick or not…. One thousand!… Shucks! Now I *know* you want him worse'n I do!" Old Man Curry hoisted the tails of his coat, thrust his hands into the hip pockets of his trousers, hunched his shoulders level with his ears and turned away.

"You ain't quitting, are you?" demanded the Sharpshooter.

"Friend," said Old Man Curry, "I ain't even started yet. It appears upon the face of the returns that you have bought one big, red hoss…. A trick hoss. To show you how I feel about it, I'm going to throw in a bridle with him…. Good-by, Elisha. The Philistines have got ye … for a thousand dollars."

It was dusk and Old Man Curry paced up and down under his stable awning, his hands clasped behind his back and his head bowed at a meditative angle. The Bald-faced Kid recalled him to earth by his breezy greeting, and what it lacked in reverence it made up in good will. Old Man Curry and the hustler were friends, each possessing trait which the other respected.

"Well, old-timer, you put airing your lace curtains a little?"

"Eh? What? Oh, good evening, Frank, good evening! I been walking up and down some. You know what it says in Ecclesiastes: 'In the day of prosperity be joyful, but in the day of adversity consider.' I been considering."

"Uh, huh," said the Bald-faced Kid, falling into step, "and you sure reached out and grabbed some adversity in that third race to-day, what? I had a finnif bet on friend Isaiah—my own money, too; that's how good I thought he was. They pretty near bumped the shoes off him in the back stretch and they had him in a pocket all the way to the paddock gate, and even so, he was only beat about the length of your nose. Adversity is right!" Old Man Curry nodded. "Say," said the Kid, lowering his voice, "I just wanted to tell you that next Tuesday the Engle bunch will be levelling with Elisha."

Curry paused in his stride and eyed the youth intently.

"Who told you?" said he.

"Never you mind," said the Kid, airily. "I'm a kind of a private information bureau and detective agency 'round this track, and my hours are from twelve to twelve, twice a day. I shake hands with the night watchman when he comes on duty and I'm here to give the milkman the high sign in the morning. They tell me things they've seen and heard. I've got a drag with the bartenders and the waiters in the track café and the telegraph operator is my pal.

"Now Engle has had Elisha for two weeks. He's started him three times and Elisha hasn't been in the money once. People are saying that when Engle bought the horse he didn't buy the prescription that goes with him…. Don't interrupt me; everybody knows you never had a hop horse in your barn…. It's my notion that Elisha can win any time they get ready to cut him loose for the kopecs. Engle has been cheating with him to get a price and using the change of owners for an alibi. They'll get their price the next time out and clean up a barrel of money. You can gamble on this tip. It's straight as gospel."

"That's pretty straight, son." Old Man Curry squared his shoulders and looked over the Kid's head toward the track, where the empty grand stand loomed dark against the evening sky. "Next Tuesday!" said he. "Just about what I thought … but tell me, son, why did you bring this to me?"

The Bald-faced Kid laughed harshly.

"Well, maybe it's because you're the only man 'round here that calls me Frank—it's my name and I like to hear it once in a while. Maybe it's because you staked me once when I was broke and didn't take my right eye for security. Maybe it's because I figure we can both get something out of it for ourselves. If Engle is going to cut a melon, we might as well have a knife in it too."

"Ah!" said Old Man Curry, and he paced the entire length of the barn before he spoke again.

"Well, you see, son, it's this way about cutting a melon. You want to be sure it ain't green … or rotten."

"Huh?"

Old Man Curry placed his hand on the Kid's shoulder.

"My boy," said he, kindly, "you make a living by—by sort of advising folks what to bet on, don't you? If they're kind of halting between two opinions, as the Book says, you sort of—help 'em out, eh!"

The Bald-faced Kid grinned broadly.

"I guess that's about the size of it," said he.

"Well, if you've got any reg'lar customers, don't invite 'em to have a slice of Engle's melon next Tuesday. It might disagree with 'em."

"But I don't see how you're going to get away from Elisha! He's fit and ready and right on edge. You can throw out his last three races. He's good enough to win without any framing."

"I know he is, son. Didn't I train him? Now you've told me something that I've been trying to find out, and I've told you something you never could find out. Don't ask me any more…. No use talking, Frank, Solomon was a great man. Some time I hope to have a race hoss fit to be named after him. I've never seen one yet."

"Where does Solomon get in on this proposition?" demanded the youth.

Old Man Curry chuckled.

"You don't read him," he said. "Solomon wrote a lot of advice that hossmen can use. For instance: 'A prudent man foreseeth the evil and hideth himself, but the simple pass on and are punished.' I've told you this Engle melon ain't as ripe as they think it is. You be prudent and don't ask me how I know."

"If the frame-up goes wrong, what'll win?" asked the Kid.

"Well," said the old man, "my hoss Elijah's in that same race, but it's a little far for him. I ain't going to bet anything. Sometimes it comes handy to know these things."

"You spoke an armful then!" said the Kid. "Well, I've got to be going. I'll keep this under my hat."

"So do, son," said Old Man Curry. "So do. Good night."

The Bald-faced Kid reflected aloud as he departed.

"And some people think that old fellow don't know the right way of the track!" he murmured. "Gee! I'd give something to be in with what he's got up his sleeve!"

Old Man Curry was still tramping up and down when little Mose returned from his nightly foray upon the crap games of the neighbourhood. The boy approached silently and with lagging gait, sure signs that fortune had not been kind to him. When the dice behaved well it was his habit to return with songs and improvised dance steps.

"Talk 'bout luck!" said he, morosely. "You know 'at flat-foot Swede whut swipes faw Mist' O'Conneh? Hungry Hanson, 'ey calls him. Well, he goes crazy 'ith 'e heat an' flang 'em bones jus' like he's got 'em ejicated. Done tossed out nine straight licks, boss. Seems to me 'at's mo' luck 'an a Swede ought to have!"

"Mose," said Old Man Curry suddenly, "Job was no hossman."

"I neveh 'cused him of it," replied Mose sulkily.

"A hossman wouldn't have wanted his adversary to write a book. If he'd said *make* a book, now … but the best way to get square with an adversary is to have him start a hoss in the same race with you, Mose."

"I'll take yo' word faw it, boss," said Mose. "When you go talkin' 'bout Job an' Sol'mun an' 'em Bible folks, you got me ridin' on a track I don't know nothin' 'bout. Nothin' a-a-atall."

It was Tuesday afternoon and little Mose was struggling into his riding boots. The other jockeys dressed in the jockeys' room at the paddock inclosure, but Mose found it pleasanter to don the silks in the tack room of Old Man Curry's barn, which also served him as a sleeping apartment. The old man sat on the edge of Mose's cot, speaking earnestly and slapping the palm of his left hand with the fingers of his right, as if to lend emphasis to his words.

"The big thing is to get him away from the post. I want Elijah out there in front when you turn for home. With his early speed, he ought to be leading into the stretch. Elisha will come from behind; Engle is smart enough for that. He'll have to pass you somewhere, because Elijah will begin to peter out after he's gone half a mile. Pull in as close to Elisha as you can, but not so close that Merritt can claim a foul, and—you know the rest."

Mose nodded soberly. "Sutny do, boss. But I neveh knowed 'at ol' 'Lisha ____"

"That'll do," said Old Man Curry sternly. "There's lots of things you don't know, Mose."

"Yes, suh," said the little negro, subsiding. "Quite a many."

Later the Bald-faced Kid came to Old Man Curry in the paddock.

"Elisha looks awful good," said he, "and they're commencing to set in the checks. He opened at 4 to 1, went up to 6, and they've hammered him down to 2 to 1 now. I hear they're playing the bulk of their money in the pool rooms all over the coast.... Elisha looks as if he could win, eh?"

Old Man Curry combed his beard.

"You can't always tell by the looks of a melon what's inside it, my son."

"Engle is telling everybody that the horse ain't quite ready," persisted the hustler. "Of course they don't want everybody betting on him and spoiling the price."

"He's doing 'em a kindly act without knowing it," said Old Man Curry. "That's 'bout the only way he'll ever do one, Frank, unbeknownst like."

"You're not betting on this one?" asked the Kid.

"Not a thin dime's worth. It's too far for him."

"I give it up." The Kid shook his head, hopelessly. "You're too many for me."

The presiding judge came out on the platform in front of the stand and watched the horses dance along the rail on their way to the post, coats glistening, eyes flashing, nostrils flaring—one of the prettiest sights the turf offers to its patrons. "Merritt on Elisha again," said the judge. "Merritt. Hm- m-m. That young man is entirely too strong in the arms to suit me. It struck me the last three times he rode this horse. But somebody is betting on Elisha to-day. That may make a difference, and if it does, we may have to ask Mr. Sharpshooter Engle a few questions."

"Leave it to him to answer 'em," said the associate judge. "It's the best thing he does. That fellow is like a hickory nut—smooth on the outside, but hard, awfully hard, to get anything out of.... Old Man Curry is in this race with Elijah. Little far for him, isn't it?"

In the very top row of the grand stand Grouchy Martin O'Connor waited for Al Engle. Just as the horses reached the post, the Sharpshooter slipped in, breathless and fumbling at the catch of his binocular case. "He was 6 to 5 when I came through the betting ring," said Engle. "Well, any old price is a good price. He'll roll home."

"He better. He owes me something," growled O'Connor.

"This is where he pays you."

"I hope so."

"I saw Old Man Curry out in the paddock," and Engle smiled at the recollection. "What do you think the old coot said to me?"

"What do I care what an old nut says?"

"Nobody cares, of course, but this was kind of funny. After the horses started for the post he came up to me, solemn as a judge, and says he: 'Remember, I told you this was a trick horse.' Just like that. They ought to have a look at his head. He's got an attic for rent, sure."

"Must have. But what does he mean by that trick-horse stuff? He pulled it on you a couple of times when you ran Elisha up on him."

"Darned if I know. I guess that's just his way of kidding…. Hello! They're off!"

"Yes, and that thing of Curry's got away flying."

"He'll quit about the time he hits the head of the stretch," said Engle. "He gets his mail there…. Merritt has got Elisha in on the rail, taking it easy, as I told him to. Believe me, that baby is some stretch runner!"

"It cost me enough to find it out!" said O'Connor shortly.

Engle peered through his binoculars.

"Unless he breaks a leg, or something"—here O'Connor hastily knocked wood—"we'll clean up," said Engle, critically. "Elisha is fighting for his head —wants to run. I don't care where he is, turning for home. He'll run over that bunch in the last quarter."

"Yes, but look at that Elijah go!" muttered O'Connor.

"Let him go!" said Engle, with a trace of irritation. "He'll come back; he always does. Bet you fifty he's last!"

"Got you!" snapped O'Connor. "You may not know any more about this one than you did about Elisha last month!"

The dots of colour skimmed around the upper turn, one of them so far ahead that it seemed lonely. This was Elijah, burning his early speed, jack-rabbiting ten lengths in front of his field, but beginning to notice his exertions and feel the swift pace.

"'Lijah," remarked little Mose, looking back over his shoulder, "if eveh you finds a race track whut's got a short home stretch in it, you'll be 'notheh Roseben. Sutny will. On'iest trouble 'ith you, 'Lijah, 'em stretches built too *long* faw you. Put 'e judges' stand up heah whah we is now, an' yo' neveh lose a race!... Uh, huh! Heah come 'Lisha now; 'em otheh jocks lettin' him th'ough on 'e rail.... Come on, honey blossom! We's waitin' faw you. Come on!"

Said the presiding judge: "That thing in front is quitting to nothing ... and here comes Elisha through on the rail.... Yes, he's a real race horse to-day. Better see Engle about this. Have to teach him that he can't run his horses in and out at this track!"

Said Al Engle: "What did I tell you? Running over horses, ain't he? He'll have that Elijah grabbed in a few more jumps.... Take it easy, Merritt! Don't win too far with him!"

Martin O'Connor heaved a great sigh of relief. Like all cautious souls, he never ceased to worry until the last doubt was dispelled. The weary, staggering Elijah was the only barrier between Elisha and the goal. O'Connor's practiced eye saw no menace in that floundering front runner; no danger in a shaft already spent. "He wins! He wins easy!" breathed Martin.

"Just rolls home, I tell you!" said the Sharpshooter, putting away his binoculars. "I knew he would."

By leaps and bounds the stretch-running Elisha overhauled his former stable companion. Poor, tired Elijah was rocking in his gait, losing ground almost as fast as Elisha was gaining it; his race was behind him; he could do no more.

Mose, keeping watch out of the tail of his eye, saw the bay head bobbing close behind. Now it was at Elijah's heels; the next stride would bring it level with the saddle.... The next stride.

All that anyone ever saw was that Jockey Moseby Jones leaned slightly toward the flying Elisha as Merritt drew alongside, and very few spectators saw this much. Who cares to watch a loser when the winner is in sight? Old Man Curry, waiting at the paddock gate, saw the movement and immediately began to search his pockets for tobacco.

Jockey Merritt, strong of arm but weak of principle, was first to realize that something had happened. Elisha's speed checked with such suddenness that the rider narrowly escaped pitching out of the saddle.... Had the horse stumbled ... or been frightened?... What in the world was it?... Merritt recovered his balance and quite instinctively drove the spurs home; the only response was a grunt from Elisha. The long racing stride shortened to a choppy one. The horse was not tired, nor was he quitting in the general acceptance of the term; he was merely stopping to a walk with all possible speed. Merritt was seized with panic. He drew his whip and began slashing savagely. Elisha answered this by waving his tail high in the air, a protest and a flag of truce—but run he would not. His pace grew slower and slower and at the paddock gate he was on even terms with the drooping Elijah. "What ails that horse?" demanded the presiding judge. "He won't run a lick! Acts as if he's taken a sulky streak all at once!"

"Yes," said the associate. "The Bible horses are having a contest to see which one of 'em can quit the fastest…. Queer-looking race, judge. And they bet on Elisha this time, too."

"I'm glad of it!" exploding the other. "It serves 'em right. I like to see a frame-up go wrong once in a while!"

Side by side Elijah and Elisha fell back toward the field, little Mose grinning from ear to ear, but industriously hand riding his mount; Jockey Merritt cursing wildly and plying rawhide and steel with all his strength. The other horses, coming on with a closing rush, enveloped the pair, passing them and continued on toward the wire.

Only one remark of Martin O'Connor's is fit for quotation. It came when his vocabulary was bare of vituperation, abusive epithet, and profanity.

"You can slip me fifty, Engle. That darned trick horse of yours was last!"

An inquisitive soul is an itching thing and the gathering of information was the Bald-faced Kid's ruling passion. He called at Old Man Curry's stable that evening with a bit of news which he hoped to use as the key to a secret.

"Greetings!" said he at the tack-room door. "Thought you'd like to know that Engle has sold Elisha. Pete Lawrence bought him for three hundred dollars. Engle says that's two-ninety-five more than he'd bring at a soap works."

Old Man Curry had been reading by the light of the tack-room lantern; he pushed his glasses back on his forehead and smiled at his informant.

"Oh, Elisha!" said he. "Yes, if you look in the second stall to the right, you'll find him. He's been straying among the publicans and sinners, but he's home again now where he belongs. I asked Pete to go over and buy him for me."

"Good work!" said the Kid, seating himself. "There's quite a mass meeting over at Engle's barn."

"So?" said Old Man Curry.

"Yes indeed! They've got Jock Merritt up on the carpet and they haven't decided yet whether to hang him to a rafter or boil him in oil. Some of 'em think he pulled Elisha to-day. Merritt is giving 'em a powerful argument. Says he never rode a harder finish in his life, but that the horse took a sudden notion to quit and did it. Didn't seem to be tired or anything, but just stopped running. O'Connor gets the floor once in a while and rips and raves about that 'trick-horse thing.' He thinks you know something. Engle says you don't and never did, but that Elisha is a dog, same as he said at first. Wouldn't surprise me none if they got into a free-for-all fight over there because they're all losers and all sore. Jock Merritt is sorer'n anybody; he bet some of his own money and he thinks they ought to give it back to him.... Now, just between friends, what happened to that horse to-day? You told me he wouldn't win, but at the head of the stretch he looked like a 1 to 10 chance. I thought he'd walk in. Then all at once he quit running. He wasn't pulled, but something stopped him and stopped him quick. What was it?"

Old Man Curry stroked his beard and regarded the Bald-faced Kid with a tolerant expression.

"Well, now," said he at length, "seeing as how you know so much, I'm going to tell you something more 'bout that 'Lisha hoss. He used to have another name once."

"Silver Star," nodded the Kid. "I looked him up in the form charts."

Old Man Curry nodded.

"Eddie Caley—him they called the Cricket—owned the hoss in the first place. Raised him from a yearling. Now understand, I ain't excusing the Cricket for what he done, and I ain't blaming him neither. He was sick most of the time, and a sick man gets his notions sort of twisted like. Maybe he figured the race track owed him something for taking away his health. I don't know. He wasn't no hand to talk.

"Anyhow, he had this one hoss and always the one idea in his head—to slip him over at such a long price that he could clean up enough to quit on. Caley was doing his own training and riding. I kept an eye on the hoss, and it seemed to me Silver Star worked good enough to win, but every time he got in a race he'd quit at the head of the stretch. That struck me as sort of queer because he come from stretch-running stock. His daddy was a great one to win from behind. Well, six or seven times Silver Star quit that way, and from the head of the stretch home the Cricket would lay into him, whip and spur both. Wouldn't make the slightest difference to the hoss, but everybody could see that Caley was doing his best to make him run. Folks got kind of sorry for him, sick that way, only one hoss and him such a dog.

"Then one day Caley came to me and wanted the loan of some money. He said the price had got long enough to suit him, but that he didn't have anything to bet. Happened I had the bank roll handy and I let him have two hundred. I can see the little feller now, with the red patches on his cheeks and his eyes kind of shining with fever.

"'This is the biggest cinch that ever came off on a race track!' he says to me, coughing every few words. 'Don't let the price scare you. Don't let anything scare you. He'll be a good hoss to-day. Win something for yourself.'

"It's this way 'bout me: I've heard that kind of talk before. When I bet, it's got to be on my own hoss. I thought two hundred was plenty to lose. Silver Star was 25 and 30 to 1 all over the ring and a friend of Caley's unloaded the two hundred in little driblets so's nobody would get suspicious and cut the price too far. The Cricket got out of a sick bed to ride the race and Silver Star came from behind and won by seven lengths. Could have made it seventeen easy as not. I reckon everybody was glad to see Caley win—everybody but the bookmakers, but they hadn't any right to kick, seeing as he beat a red-hot favourite.

"Caley went to bed that night and didn't get up any more. I used to read to him when he couldn't sleep. Maybe that's how he come to give me the hoss, along with a little secret 'bout him."

Old Man Curry paused, tantalisingly, and rummaged in his pockets for his fine-cut. The Bald-faced Kid squirmed on his chair.

"It was a trick that nobody but a jockey would ever have thought of, son. Caley taught the colt to stop whenever a certain word was hollered in his ear. Dinged it into him, morning after morning, until Silver Star got so's he'd quit as soon as he heard it, like a buggy hoss stops when you say 'Whoa' to him. Best part of the trick, though, was that all the whipping and spurring in the world couldn't get him to running again. Caley taught him that for his own protection. It gave him an alibi with the judges. Couldn't they see he was riding the hoss as hard as he knew how? I don't say it was exackly *honest*, but ——."

"Oho!" interrupted the Bald-faced Kid, "now I know why you had a front runner in that race! Between friends, old-timer, what was it Mose hollered at Elisha when he came alongside?"

"Well," said Old Man Curry, "that's the secret of it, my son, and it's this way 'bout a secret: you can't let too many folks in on it. I reckon it was a word spoken in due season, as Solomon says. Elisha, he won't hear it again unless he changes owners."

⸻

PLAYING EVEN FOR OBADIAH

Old Man Curry, owner of race horses, looked out of his tack-room door at a streaming sky and gave thanks for the rain. Other owners were cursing the steady downpour, for a wet track would sadly interfere with their plans, but Curry expected to start the chestnut colt Obadiah that afternoon, and Obadiah, as Jockey Moseby Jones was wont to remark, was a mud-running fool on any man's track. The Bald-faced Kid, who lived by doing the best he could and preferred to be called a hustler rather than a tout, spoke from the tack-room interior. He was a privileged character at the Curry barn.

"How does she look, old-timer? Going to clear up by noon?"

Old Man Curry shook his head. "Well, no," said he. "I reckon not. Looks to me like reg'lar Noah weather, Frank. If a man's got a mud hoss in his barn, now's the time to start him."

The Bald-faced Kid grunted absently. He was deep in a thick, leather-backed, looseleaf volume of past performances, technically known as a form book, generally mentioned as "the dope sheets"—the library of the turf follower, the last resort and final court of appeal. The Kid's lower lip had a studious droop and the pages rustled under his nervous fingers. An unlighted cigarette was behind his ear.

"What you looking for, son?"

"I'm trying to make Gaspargoo win his race to-day. He's in there with a feather on his back, and there'll be a price on him. He's been working good, too. He quits on a dry track, but in the mud he's liable to go farther. His old feet won't get so hot." Curry peered over the Kid's shoulder at the crowded columns of figures and footnotes, unintelligible to any but the initiated, and supposedly a complete record of the racing activities of every horse in training.

"Hm-m-m. Some folks say Solomon didn't write Ecclesiastes. Some say he did—after he got rid of his wives."

The Bald-faced Kid laughed.

"You and your Solomon! Well, get it off your chest! What does he say now?"

"I think it must have been Solomon, because here's something that sounds just like him: 'Of making many books there is no end; and much study is a weariness of the flesh.' It would weary a mule's flesh to study them dope books, Frank. There's so many things enter into the running of hosses which ought to be printed in 'em and ain't. For instance, take that race right in front of you." The old man put his finger upon the page. "I remember it well. Here's Engle's mare, Sunflower, the favourite and comes fourth. Ab Mears wins it with the black hoss, Anthracite. Six to one. What does the book say 'bout Sunflower's race?"

The Kid read the explanatory footnote.

"'Sunflower, away badly, and messed about the first part of the journey; had no chance to catch the leaders, but closed strong under the whip.'"

"Uh-huh," said Old Man Curry. "Good as far as it goes, but that's all. Might as well tell a lie as part of the truth. Why not come right out with it and say that Engle was betting on Anthracite that day and the boy on Sunflower rode the mare to orders? That's what happened. Engle and Mears and O'Connor and Weaver and some of the rest of 'em run these races the night before over in O'Connor's barn. They get together and then decide on a caucus nominee. Why not put that in the book?"

"Speaking of Mears," said the Bald-faced Kid, "he thinks he'll win to-day with Whitethorn."

"Well," said the old man, "I'll tell you, Frank; it's this way 'bout Whitethorn; he'll win if he can beat Obadiah. The colt's ready and this weather suits him down to the ground. He surely does love to run in the slop. Only bad thing 'bout it, Engle and Weaver are both in that race, and since I trimmed that gang of pirates with Elisha they've had it in for me. Their jockeys act like somebody's told 'em there's an open season on my hosses. They bump that little nigger of mine every chance they get. Pretty near put him into the fence twice last week."

"Why don't you holler to the judges?"

"They haven't done any real damage, son. And here's another angle: these judges won't give a nigger any the best of it on a claim of foul agin a white boy. My Mose is the only darky rider here, and the other boys want to drive him out. Between Engle and his gang after me, and the jockeys after Mose, we got our hands full."

"I'll bet. Going to gamble any on Obadiah to-day?"

"If I like the price. None of the bookmakers here will ever die of enlargement of the heart. If Obadiah is shorter than three to one, he'll run for the purse alone. The hoss that beats him on a sloppy track will know that he's been going some."

It happened just beyond the half-mile pole, in a sudden flurry of wind and rain. The spectators, huddling under the grand-stand roof, saw the horses dimly as through a heavy mist. The colours were indistinguishable at the distance, drenched and sodden.

"Hello!" said the presiding judge, who had been wiping his field glasses. "One of 'em went down! What happened?"

"Don't know," replied the associate judge. "I was watching that thing in front —Whitethorn.... Yes, and that horse is hurt, Major.... The boy is all right, though. He's on his feet."

"It's Old Man Curry's horse," said the other. "Obadiah—and I sort of figured him the contender in this race, too.... The boy has got him.... Looks like a broken leg to me.... Too bad.... Better send an officer over there."

Before the judges knew that anything had happened a shabby, bearded old man in a rusty black frock coat dodged across the track from the paddock gate and splashed hurriedly through the infield. Old Man Curry never used binoculars; he had the eyes of an eagle.

"Been looking for it to happen every day!" he muttered. "And a right likely colt, too. The skunks! The miserable little skunks!"

Whitethorn, the winner of the race, was back in the ring and unsaddled before the old man reached the half-mile pole. Jockey Moseby Jones, plastered with mud from his bullet head to his boots, shaken and bruised but otherwise unhurt, clung to Obadiah's bridle.

"Now, honey, you jus' stan' still!" he was saying. "Jus' stan' still an' we git yo' laig fixed up in no time; no time a-a-a-tall."

The colt stood with drooping head, drumming on the ground with the crippled foreleg; from time to time the unfortunate animal shivered as with a violent chill. Old Man Curry knelt in the mud, but rose almost immediately; one glance at the broken leg was enough. He looked at the little negro.

"How did it happen, Mose?"

"Jockey Murphy done it, boss. He was on 'at thing of Weaver's."

"A-purpose?"

"Sutny he done it a-purpose. He cut in on us an' knocked us agin the rail. Come from 'way outside to do it."

Old Man Curry began to take the saddle off the colt. A tall man in a rubber coat, gum boots, and a uniform cap arrived on the scene, panting after his run from the grand stand. He looked at Obadiah's leg, sucked in his breath with a whistling sound more expressive than words, and faced Old Man Curry.

"Want the 'vet' to see him?" asked the newcomer.

"No use in him suffering that long," said the old man dully. "He's ruined. Might as well get it over with."

Jockey Moseby Jones wailed aloud.

"Oh, don' let 'em shoot Obadiah, boss!" he pleaded. "I'll take keer o' him; I'll set up nights 'ith him. Can't you splint it? Ain't there nothin' we kin do fo' him?"

"Only one thing, Mose," said Old Man Curry. "It's a kindness, I reckon." He passed the bridle to the uniformed stranger. "Don't be too long about it," said he.

The colt, gentle and obedient to the last, hobbled off the track toward a sheltering grove of trees near the upper turn. Custom decrees that the closing scene of a turf tragedy shall not be enacted within sight of the grand stand. Two very young stableboys followed at a distance.

"Run away, kids," said the tall man, fumbling at his hip pocket. "You don't want to see this."

Old Man Curry strode along the track, his shoulders squared, his face stern and his eyes blazing with the cold rage which sometimes overtakes a patient man. Little Mose trailed at his heels, whimpering and casting scared glances behind. After a time they heard the muffled report of a pistol.

"He's out of his misery, sonny," said the old man. "It's the best way—the best way—and now I want you to tell them judges just how it happened."

But Jockey Murphy had already told his story, ably seconded by his friends, Grogan and Merritt. These boys had been interviewed by racing judges before and, consequently, were not embarrassed.

"Judges—gentlemen," said Murphy, cap in hand—a vest-pocket edition of a horseman, freckled, blue-eyed, and bow-legged—"this was how it happened: That little nigger nearly spilled the whole bunch of us, tryin' to cut acrost to the rail goin' into the turn. We yelled at him, and he kind of lost his head— tried to yank his hoss around and down he went. Awful slippery over there, judges. I had to pull up with Fieldmouse, and couldn't get her to going again. She's a mean, skulking mare, and won't run a lick after she's been interfered with.... Who else saw it? Why, Merritt was right there somewheres, and so was Grogan. They're all that I'm sure of. You might ask 'em whether the nigger cut acrost or not. He's an awful reckless little kid, and he'll kill somebody yet if he ain't more careful."

Grogan and Merritt, called in support of this statement, perjured themselves like jockeys, and there was no conflicting note in the testimony. Mose, coming late, told his story, but the judges were swayed by the preponderance of evidence. It was three against one, and that one a very poor witness, for Mose was overawed by his surroundings and contradicted himself several times out of pure fright. In the end he was allowed to go with a solemn warning to be more careful in the future.

When this word was brought to Old Man Curry he lumbered heavily up the steps and into the judges' stand, where he refused a chair and delivered himself standing, the water dripping in tiny puddles from the skirt of his long black coat.

"Gentlemen," said he, "you're barking up the wrong tree. I've been expecting something like this ever since the meeting opened. My little boy can't ride a race 'thout interference from these rascals that take their orders from Engle and his bunch. They've tried a dozen times to put him over the fence, and now they've killed a good hoss for me. I ain't going to stand it. I——"

"But the other boys all say——"

"Great King!" interrupted the old man wrathfully. "Of course they do! Told you the same identical story, didn't they? Ain't that proof they're lying? Did you ever see three honest people that could agree when they was trying to tell the truth 'bout an accident? Did you?"

Quite naturally the judges were inclined to regard this as a reflection upon their official conduct. Old Man Curry was reprimanded for his temerity, and descended from the stand, his beard fairly bristling with righteous indignation. Little Mose followed him down the track toward the paddock; he had to trot to keep up with the old man's stride.

"Might have knowed they'd team up agin us," said the negro. "Them Irish jockeys had a story all cooked to tell."

Old Man Curry did not open his mouth until he reached his tack-room, and then it was only to stuff one cheek with fine-cut tobacco—his solace in times of stress. After reflection he spoke, dropping his words slowly, one by one.

"Weaver and Murphy and Engle.... It says in Ecclesiastes that a threefold cord is not easily broken, but I reckon it might be done, one cord at a time.... Well, Mose, they've made us take the medicine!"

"Sutny did!" chirped the little negro. "But they'll never git us to lick the spoon!"

The Bald-faced Kid often boasted that everybody's business was his business —a large contract on any race track of the Jungle Circuit. His stop watch told him what the horses were doing, and stableboys, bartenders, and waiters told him what their owners were doing, the latter vastly more important to the Kid. At all times he used his eyes, which were sharp as gimlets. Thus it happened that he was able to give Old Man Curry a bit of interesting information.

"Considering what these birds, Weaver and Murphy, did to you last week," said the Kid, "I don't suppose you'd fight a bulldog for 'em, or anything like that?"

"Eh? What bulldog?" Old Man Curry could never keep abreast of the vernacular.

"Getting down to cases," said the Kid, "you're laying for Weaver and Murphy, ain't you?"

"I ain't said so in that many words," was the cautious response.

"You ain't going to let 'em kill a good colt for you and get away with it, are you? Weaver was only in that race to take care of Obadiah. Eagle's gang was down hook, line, and sinker on Whitethorn, and they cleaned up. Obadiah was the one they was leery of, so Weaver put Fieldmouse in the race and told Murphy to take care of you. It's simple as A, B, C. Wouldn't you get back at 'em if you had a chance?"

"I ain't signed any peace documents as I know of," said the old man, a smouldering light in his eye.

"Now you're talking!" said the Kid. "If you want to catch Weaver and Murphy dead to rights, I can tell how to go about it."

"So do, Frank," said Old Man Curry. "So do. My ear is open to your cry."

"In the first place," said the Kid, lighting a cigarette, "I don't suppose you know that Weaver has been stealing weight off his horses ever since this meeting opened."

"With Parker, the clerk of the scales?" ejaculated the old man. "I've heard that couldn't be done."

The Bald-faced Kid chuckled.

"A smart owner can do anything," said he, "and Weaver's smart. At these other tracks, stealing weight off a horse is the king of indoor sports, and they mostly work it through a stand-in with the clerk of the scales; but you're right about this fellow Parker. He's on the level, and they can't get at him. A jock has got to weigh in and weigh out on the dot when Parker is on the job. He won't let 'em get by with the difference of an ounce."

"Then how——" began Old Man Curry.

"There you go, busting through the barrier! Weaver is pulling the wool over Parker's eyes. Now here's what I saw yesterday: Weaver had Exmoor in the third race, supposed to be carrying one hundred and ten pounds. Jock Murphy ain't much bigger'n a rabbit—tack and all, he won't weigh ninety-five. That would make, say, fifteen pounds of lead in the weight pad. Murphy got on the scales and was checked out of the jock's room at one hundred and ten, all square enough, but when Weaver saddled Exmoor he left the weight pad off him entirely—slipped it to that big nigger swipe of his—Chicken Liver Pete, they call him."

"I know him," said Old Man Curry.

"Everybody knows him," said the Kid. "Well, Chicken Liver put the weight pad under the blanket that he was carrying to throw over the horse after the race. Exmoor won yesterday, but he didn't carry an ounce of lead."

"But how did Murphy make the weight after he finished?" demanded the old man.

"Easiest thing in the world!" said the Kid. "While Murphy was unsaddling the horse, Chicken Liver was right at his elbow, and both of 'em had their backs to the judges. It looked natural enough for the nigger to be there—waiting to blanket the horse the minute the saddle came off of him. All Murphy had to do was grab under the blanket with one hand while he jerked the saddle off the horse with the other—and there he was, ready to weigh one hundred and ten. I'll bet those two fellows have rehearsed that switch a thousand times. They pulled it off so slick that if I hadn't been watching for it I could have been looking right at 'em and never noticed it. And the judges didn't have the chance that I did, because they couldn't see anything but their backs. Murphy pranced in, hopped on the scales, got the O. K., and that was all there was to it. Pretty little scheme, ain't it? And so darned simple!"

Old Man Curry combed his beard with both hands—with him a sign of deep thought.

"Frank," said he at length, "where does this Chicken Liver nigger go while the race is being run?"

"Across the track to the infield. That was where he went yesterday. I was watching him."

"The infield.... Hm-m-m.... Thank you, Frank."

"You could tip it off to the judges," suggested the Kid, "and they'd have Chicken Liver searched. Like as not they'd rule Weaver off for life and set Murphy down——"

"There's a better way than searching that nigger," said Old Man Curry.

"You'll have to show me!"

"Son," said the aged owner, "according to Solomon—and, oh, what a racing judge he would have made!—'he that hath knowledge spareth his words.' I'm sparing mine for the present, but that won't keep me from doing a heap of thinking.... Engle, Weaver, and Murphy.... Maybe I can bust two of these cords at once—and fray the other one a little."

Four men sat under the lantern in Martin O'Connor's tack-room on a Wednesday night. They spoke in low tones, for they were engaged in running the fourth race on Thursday's programme.

"I've let it be known in a few places where it'll do the most good that the mare can't pack a hundred and fifteen pounds and win at a mile." This was Weaver speaking, a small, wiry man with a drooping moustache. "You know how talk gets around on a race track—tell the right man and you might as well rent the front page of the morning paper. As a matter of fact, Fieldmouse *can't* pack that weight and win."

"That's the way the form students will dope it out," said Al Engle, otherwise the Sharpshooter, the smiling, youthful, gold-toothed blond who directed the campaigns and dictated the policy of the turf pirates. "That much weight will stop most of 'em, but let her in there under ninety pounds and Fieldmouse is a cinch. That little sleight-of-hand stunt between Murphy and your nigger is working fine. They not only put it over on the judges, but none of the other owners are wise. I'd try it myself some day if I wasn't afraid somebody would fumble and give the snap away."

"Huh!" growled the saturnine O'Connor. "Needn't worry about tipping anything off to them judges. They're both blind. Here's what bothers me: Old Man Curry is in that same race with Isaiah."

"Well, what of that?" said Engle. "That old fool is all same as a nightmare to you, ain't he?"

"Call him a fool if you want to," was the stubborn rejoinder, "but he made an awful sucker out of you with that trick horse of his. An awful sucker. If Old

Man Curry is a fool, there's a lot of wise people locked up in the bug houses. That's all I've got to say!"

"He's had your goat ever since the meeting opened," grinned the Sharpshooter.

"That's all right," said O'Connor. "That's a whole lot better than my buying a goat from him—for a thousand dollars." This by way of reminding the Sharpshooter of something which he preferred to forget. Engle reddened.

"Aw, what's the good of chewing the fat?" interrupted the fourth man briskly. This was Ab Mears, of whom it was said that he trained his horses to look into the betting ring on their way to the post and to run in accordance with the figures they saw upon the bookmakers' slates. "Let's not have any arguments, boys. All little pals together, eh?... Now, getting down to business, as the fellow said when he was digging the well, Isaiah is a pretty shifty old selling plater when he's at himself; but you know and I know that the best day he ever saw he couldn't beat Fieldmouse at a mile with a feather on her back. She'll walk home alone. The most Isaiah can do is to come second——"

"He'll be lucky if he does that well," interrupted Engle. "The mare will be in front of him all the way.... Same old stuff; wait for the closing betting. Weaver, you keep on hollering your head off about the weight; it'll scare the outsiders and they won't play her. Then, at the last minute, cut loose and load up the books with all they'll take."

"Just the same," muttered O'Connor, "I'd feel a lot more comfortable if Curry wasn't in the race. That old boy is poison, that's what he is. The last couple of times——"

"Oh, shut up!" rasped Engle. "Elisha was the horse he trimmed us with—Elisha! Get that through your head. This is Isaiah. There's as much difference in horses as there is in prophets. What you need is one of those portable Japanese foot warmers."

The paddock is the place to go for information, particularly after the saddling bell rings. The owners are usually on exhibition at that time. Nearly every owner will answer a civil question about his horse; once in a great while one of them may answer truthfully. In this particular race we are concerned with but two owners, one of whom told the truth.

Weaver, rat-eyed and furtive, answered all questions freely—almost too freely.

"Ye-es, she's a right nice little mare, but they've weighted her out of it to-day. She can't pack a hundred and fifteen and win.... That much lead will stop a stake horse. Better stay off her to-day. Some other time."

Old Man Curry, grave and polite, also answered questions.

"Isaiah? Oh, yes. Well, now, sir, I'll tell you 'bout this hoss of mine. I figure he's got a stavin' good chance to come second—a stavin' good chance…. No, he won't be first."

Just before the bugle blew, Mose received his riding orders.

"If that mare of Weaver's gets away in front, don't you start chasing her. No use in running Isaiah's head off trying to ketch her. I want you to finish second, understand? Isaiah can beat all these other hosses. Don't pay no 'tention to the mare. Let her go."

Little Mose nodded.

"'At Fieldmouse is sutny a goin' fool when 'ey bet stable money on huh," said he. "Let 'at ole mare go, eh?"

"Exackly," said the old man, "but be sure you beat the rest of 'em."

"Fieldmouse an' Murphy," said Mose. "Huh-uh! 'At's a bad combination fo' us, boss, a ba-ad combination. 'Membeh Obadiah?"

The Bald-faced Kid strolled into Isaiah's stall.

"Chicken Liver's got it," he whispered. "I saw Weaver pass it to him."

"That's what I've been waiting for, Frank," said Old Man Curry. "Here, Shanghai! You lead him out on the track. I've got business with the children of Israel."

The Fieldmouse money was beginning to pour into the ring, and the block men were busy with their erasers. Each time the mare's price went down, Isaiah's price went up a little. Old Man Curry drew out a tattered roll of currency and went from booth to booth, betting on his horse at four to one.

"Think you've got a chance to-day, old man?" It was the Sharpshooter, smiling like a cherub.

"Well, now," said Curry, "I'll tell you 'bout me; I'm always trying, so I've always got a chance. Looks like the weight ought to stop the mare."

"That's so," said Engle. "Betting much?"

"Quite considerable for me, yes. Isaiah ain't a trick hoss, but he——"

"Oh, you go to the devil!" said Engle.

But Old Man Curry crossed the track instead. His first care was to locate the negro known as Chicken Liver; this done, he watched the start of the race. Nine horses were lined up at the barrier, and at least six of the jockeys were manœuvring for a flying start. The official starter, a thick-set man with a long twisted nose, bellowed loudly from time to time.

"No! No! You can't break that way!… You, Murphy! I'll fine you in a minute!… Get back there, Grogan! What did I tell you, Murphy?… Bring that horse up slow! *Bring him up!* No! No! You can't break that way!"

Isaiah stood perfectly still in the middle of the track; on either side of him the nervous animals charged at the barrier or whirled away from it in sudden, wild dashes. The starter's voice grew husky and his temper hot, but at last the horses were all headed in the right direction, if only for the fraction of a second. Jockey Murphy, scenting a start, had Fieldmouse in motion even as the elastic webbing shot into the air; she was in her racing stride as the starter's voice blared out:

"You're off! Go on! *Go on!*"

The mare, always a quick breaker, rushed into the lead, Murphy taking her on an easy slant to the inner rail. Isaiah, swinging a bit wide on the first turn, settled down to work, and at the half-mile pole was leading the pursuit, taking the dust which Fieldmouse kicked up five lengths in front.

Chicken Liver, watching Murphy skim the rail into the home stretch, shuffled his feet in an ecstasy of exultation.

"Come home, baby!" he shouted. "Come 'long home! You de bes' li'l ole hawss—*uh!*"

Something small and hard jammed violently into the pit of Chicken Liver's stomach, and his song of victory ended in an amazed grunt. Old Man Curry was glaring at him and pressing the muzzle of a forty-five-calibre revolver against the exact spot where the third button of Chicken Liver's vest would have been had he owned such a garment.

"Drop that weight pad, nigger, or I'll blow you inside out! *Drop it!*"

Chicken Liver leaped backward with a howl of terror. The next instant he was well on his way to the Weaver barn, supplication floating over his shoulder.

"Don't shoot, misteh! Fo' de Lawd's sake, don't shoot!"

Old Man Curry picked up the weight pad and started for the gate. He arrived in time to see the smile on Murphy's face as he swung under the wire, three lengths in front of Isaiah, the other horses trailing far in the rear. Murphy was still smiling broadly when he brought Fieldmouse back into the chalked circle, a privileged space reserved for winners.

"Judges!" piped the jockey shrilly, touching the visor of his cap with his whip. Receiving the customary nod, Murphy slid to the ground and attacked the cinch. It was then that Chicken Liver should have stepped forward with his blanket—then that the deft transfer should have taken place, but Chicken Liver, where was he? Murphy's anxious eyes travelled around the wide circle of owners and hostlers, and his smile faded into a nervous grin.

Now, after each race a few thousand impatient people must wait for the official announcement—the one, two, three, without which no tickets can be cashed—and the official announcement must wait upon the weighing of the riders. For this reason no time is wasted in the ceremony.

"Hurry up, son," said the presiding judge. "We're waiting on you."

Murphy fumbled with the strap, playing desperately for time. As he tugged, his eyes were searching for the missing negro. He caught one glimpse of Weaver's face, yellow where it was not white; he, too, was raking the horizon for Chicken Liver.

"What's the matter with you, Murphy?" demanded the judge. "Do you want help with that tack?"

"No, sir," faltered the jockey. "Th-this thing sticks somehow. I'll git it in a minute. I——"

Old Man Curry marched through the ring and up the steps to the platform of the judges' stand, and when Weaver saw what he carried in his hand he became a very sick man indeed—and looked it. Al Engle backed away into the crowd and Martin O'Connor followed him, mumbling incoherently.

"Maybe this is what Murphy is waiting for, judges," said Old Man Curry with marked cheerfulness. "Maybe he don't want to git on the scales without it."

"Eh?" said the presiding judge. "What is that?"

"Looks like a weight pad to me," said Old Man Curry, "with quite a mess of lead in it. Yes, it *is* a weight pad."

"Where did you get it?"

"Well," said the old man, "I'll tell you 'bout that: Weaver's nigger had it smuggled under a blanket, but he dropped it and I picked it up. Maybe Weaver thought the nigger was a better weight packer than the mare. I don't know. Maybe——"

"Young man," commanded the presiding judge, "that'll do you. Take your tackle and get on the scales. Lively now!"

Murphy cast one despairing glance about him and slouched to his undoing. The judge, weight pad in hand, followed him into the weighing room underneath the stand. He was back again almost instantly, and his voice had an angry ring.

"Change those numbers!" said he. "The mare is disqualified. Isaiah, first; Rainbow, second; put the fourth horse third. Mr. Weaver, come up here, sir! And where's that nigger? I want him too. Murphy, I'll see you later…. Don't go away, Mr. Curry. I need you."

"That's what I call getting hunk with a vengeance, old-timer." Thus the Bald-faced Kid, at the door of Old Man Curry's tack-room. "You cleaned up right, didn't you? Weaver's ruled off for life, and his horses with him—he can't even sell 'em to another stable. Murphy's lost his license. Chicken Liver's out of a job. Engle and his bunch are in the clear, but they lost a lot of money on the mare. Regular old blunderbuss, ain't you? Didn't miss anybody."

"Son," said Old Man Curry, removing his spectacles, "Solomon had it right. He says: 'Whoso diggeth a pit shall fall therein.' Weaver dug one big enough to hold his entire stable. And that reminds me: I bet fifty dollars for you to-day, and here's the two hundred. Run it up if you can, but remember what Solomon says about that: 'He that maketh haste to be rich shall not be innocent.'"

"I'll take a chance," said the Bald-faced Kid, reaching for the money.

———————

BY A HAIR

"Son," said Old Man Curry, "what's on your mind besides your hat? You ain't said a word for as much as two minutes, and any time you keep still that long there must be something wrong."

The Bald-faced Kid's glance rested for an instant upon the kindly features of the patriarch of the Jungle Circuit, then flickered away down the line of stables where other horsemen and race-track followers were sunning themselves and waiting the summons to the noon meal.

Old Man Curry, his eyes half closed, a straw in the corner of his mouth, and the brim of his slouch hat resting upon the bridge of his nose, seemed not to be conscious of this brief but piercing scrutiny. As usual with him, there was about this venerable person a beguiling air of innocence and confidence in his fellow man, a simple attitude of trustfulness not entirely borne out by his method of handling a racing stable. Certain dishonest horsemen and bookmakers were beginning to suspect that Old Man Curry was smarter than he looked. The Bald-faced Kid had never entertained any doubts upon this subject. He remained silent, the thin edge of a grin playing about his lips.

"I hope you ain't been trying to show any tinhorn gamblers the error of their ways by ruining 'em financially," said the old man, one drowsy eye upon the Kid's face. "That's one of the things what just naturally can't be done. Steady growth is the thing to fat a bank roll, Frank. I'm about to tell you how you can multiply yours considerable. Last time you was here you had two hundred dollars, spoiled Egyptian money——"

"Oh, I guess it wasn't so darn badly spoiled at that!" interrupted the Kid. "I didn't have any trouble getting rid of it." He grinned sheepishly. "Your friend Solomon called the turn on the get-rich-quick stuff. 'He that maketh haste'— what's the rest of it, old-timer?"

"'He that maketh haste to be rich shall not be innocent,'" quoted Old Man Curry, rolling out the syllables in sonorous procession. "But I reckon not being rich is worrying you more than not being innocent. Who took the roll away from you?"

"Squeaking Henry got a piece of it," admitted the Kid. "Did you ever play twenty-one—Black Jack, old-timer?"

Old Man Curry shook his head.

"I never monkeyed much with cards," said he, "but I've seen the game played some—when I was younger."

"Well," said the Kid mournfully, "Squeaking Henry and a couple of his friends rung in some marked cards—on my deal. Of course those burglars could take one flash at the top of the deck and know just when to draw and when not to. I sat up there like a flathead and let 'em clean me. What tipped it off was that when I was down to my last smack, with a face card in sight and a face card in the hole, Henry drew to twenty and caught an ace. The mangy little crook! Oh, well, easy come, easy go. I'd have lost it some other way, I guess. But, say, what was this proposition of yours about fattening the bank roll? I've got seven dollars between me and the wolf, and he's so close that I can smell his breath."

"Seeing that you ain't got any more judgment than that," was Old Man Curry's comment, "I don't know as I ought to tell you."

"Oh, all right," said the Kid, "if that's the way you feel about it—but maybe I've got some information I could trade you for it."

"I never swapped hosses blind," said Old Man Curry.

"I won't ask you to," said the Bald-faced Kid. "It's no news that Engle's bunch is out for your scalp, is it?"

"No-o," said the old man. "I kind of suspicioned as much."

"They're after you strong, old-timer. First you walloped 'em with Elisha, then you double-crossed 'em with Elijah, and then you got Weaver and Murphy ruled off. At first Engle thought you was only ignorant but shot full of blind luck. Lately he ain't been so sure about the ignorance. Engle hates to give anybody else credit for being wise to the angles around this track."

"Solomon said something about him," remarked Old Man Curry gravely.

"Go ahead; pull it!" said the Kid.

"'Seest thou a man wise in his own conceit? There is more hope of a fool than of him.' That's what Solomon thought about the Engle family, son."

"Well, if I was you I wouldn't lay any fancy odds that Engle is a fool," warned the Kid. "There's one baby that you've got to figure on every minute. You've got a horse in your barn that Engle is watching like a hawk."

"Elisha?"

"Elisha. When does he start the next time?"

"In the Handicap."

"The Handicap, eh? You must think pretty well of him. Some good horses in that race. Well, there won't be a price on him worth taking; you can bet on that."

Old Man Curry opened his eyes wide for the first time.

"No price on him! Nonsense! He's a selling plater going up agin so-called stake horses! No price! Huh!"

"Even so, nevertheless, notwithstanding, and but," said the Kid with exasperating calmness, "you won't get a price on him. I can quote some myself. The voice of wisdom is speaking to you."

"But he ain't never done anything that would justify starting him with stake hosses," argued Old Man Curry, feeling in his pockets for his fine-cut.

"Is there any law to prevent 'em figuring that he might?"

"But why is Engle worrying about the price on my hosses?" demanded Curry.

"Maybe to get even for what you've done to him. Maybe because he's got some sort of an agreement with Abe Goldmark. You know Abe?"

"By sight, son, by sight. And that's the only way I want to know him."

"You and me both," said the Kid quickly. "I don't like that fellow's face or the way he wears it, but you can't afford to overlook him any more than you can overlook a rattlesnake. Goldmark is another one of the wise boys. He runs one book, but he's under cover with an interest in five or six more. He comes pretty near being a combination in restraint of trade, Goldmark does. The Handicap is going to be the big betting race of the meeting. Goldmark has been tipped to keep his eye out for Elisha. On Elisha's record he ought to be 15 or 20 to 1."

"Longer than that!" said Old Man Curry.

"I'm figuring these syndicate books," said the Kid. "He'll open around 3 to 1 and stay there whether there's a dollar bet on him or not. False odds? Certainly, but they're taking no chances on you. They figure you won't be trying at that price. And another thing: This same Squeaking Henry, this marked-card gambler, has gone to work for Goldmark. Three dollars a day for what he can find out. Is this information worth anything to you?"

"It might be, son," said Old Man Curry. "It might be. I'll let you know later on."

"On the level," said the Kid, "you don't figure that Elisha has got a chance to win that race—not with Regulator and Black Bill and Miss Amber in it? They're no Salvators, I admit, still they're the best we ever see in this part of the country. Black Bill is a demon over a distance, old-timer. He won that two-mile race last winter at Santa Anita. Elisha has never gone more than a mile and an eighth, and this is a mile and a half. Honest, now, you don't think he can beat horses like Black Bill and Regulator, do you?"

"Son," said Old Man Curry, "I never think anything about a race until the night before. That's time enough."

"But suppose they make him a short price? You wouldn't cut him loose and let him make a showing that would spoil him as a betting proposition?"

"Well, maybe he won't be a short price," said the old man. "You can't tell a thing about it. It's this way with bookmakers: Once in a while they change their minds, and that's where an honest hossman gets a crack at 'em. Yes, they get to fooling with their little pieces of chalk. I don't reckon Elisha will be less'n 20 to 1. There goes the gong at the boarding house. Might as well eat with me and nurse that seven dollars all you can."

The Bald-faced Kid rose with alacrity and bowed low, his hand upon his heart.

"You are the ideal host," said he, "and I am the ideal hostee! I could eat a horse and chase the driver. Lead the way, old-timer!"

The money which Squeaking Henry won by reason of the marked cards did him very little good, remaining in his possession barely long enough to cause his vest pocket to sag a trifle. He lost it in a friendly game with the friends who were clever enough to plan the raid on the Bald-faced Kid's bank roll, using Henry as a tool, much as the coastwise Chinaman uses a cormorant in his fishing operations. Stripped of his opulence, Squeaking Henry found himself flat on the market again.

Henry was a tout, hence an easy and extemporaneous liar, but, alas, a clumsy one. He lacked the Bald-faced Kid's finesse; lacked also his tireless energy, his insatiable curiosity, and the thin vein of pure metal which lay underneath the base. There was nothing about Squeaking Henry which was not for sale cheap; body and soul, he was on life's bargain counter among the remnants, and Abe Goldmark, examining the lot, found a price tag labelled three dollars a day.

"Uh-huh," said Henry. "I get you, Mr. Goldmark. You want me to stick around Old Man Curry's barn and pump him."

"Never mind the pumping," said Goldmark. "The less you talk and the fewer questions you ask the better. Curry is no fool, understand. He might be just as smart as you are. Judging by the number of good things he's put over at this meeting, he's smarter. I want to know who calls on him, who his stable connections are, who he——"

"Aw, he ain't got no stable connections!" said Squeaking Henry in great disgust. "He plays the game alone, and when he wants to bet he walks into the ring and goes to it. Never had a betting commissioner in his life, and if you want to know when the stable money is down, all you've got to do is watch Curry. Cinch!"

"Oh, a cinch is it?" sneered Goldmark. "Then I'm making a big mistake to hire you to find out things. You know everything already, eh?"

"Well, I guess not *everything*," mumbled the abashed Henry.

"That's my guess, too!" snapped Goldmark. "I'm paying you to watch that Curry stable; get me? And I want you to *watch* it! I want to know everything that happens around there from now on, understand? Particularly, I want a line on this Elisha horse. Know him when you see him?"

"S-s-sure!" said Squeaking Henry. "Sure I do! Big, leggy bay with a white spot on his forehead about the size of a nickel. Do I know him? Well!"

"I want to know when Curry works him—how far and how fast. I want to know what the old man thinks of his chances in the Handicap. You can get me at the hotel every night after dinner. Better use the telephone. In case you slip up or miss me, send word by Al Engle."

"All right," said Henry.

"And say," Goldmark actually grinned, "I hear this Curry is a soft-hearted old fellow. Why couldn't you tell him a hard-luck story and get to sleep in his tack-room nights? Then you'd be right on the ground. Try a hard-luck story on him. The one you sprang on me wasn't so bad."

"H-m-m-m," mused Henry. "I might, and that's a fact. He ain't a bad guy, Old Man Curry ain't. He stakes the hustlers every once in a while."

"Well," said Goldmark insinuatingly, "if he should be such a sucker as to stake you, don't forget you was on my pay roll *first*; that's all I ask."

"Aw, whadda you take me for?" growled Squeaking Henry, virtuously indignant at the barest hint of duplicity. "I ain't that kind of a guy."

Since the tout lives by his wits and his tongue, he is never without a hard-luck story—a dependable one, tried, but seldom, if ever, true. He circles human nature, searching for the weak point and, having found it, delivers the attack. Squeaking Henry knew the armour plate to be thinnest on man's sympathetic side, and the hard-luck story which he told Old Man Curry would have melted the heart of a golf club handicapper. The story was overworked and threadbare in spots, but it brought an immediate result.

"And that's how I'm fixed," whined Squeaking Henry in conclusion. "I think I can rustle the eats all right enough—one meal a day anyway—and if I just had a place to sleep——" He paused and regarded Old Man Curry expectantly.

"Come in, son," said the patriarch. A wiser man than Squeaking Henry might have found Curry's manner almost too friendly. "Come in. There's a spare cot here and you're welcome to it. Mose, my little nigger, sleeps here too, but I reckon you won't mind him. He's clean."

Strange to say, it was Jockey Moseby Jones who minded. He minded very much, in plain English, waylaying Old Man Curry as he made the rounds of the stalls that night, lantern in hand.

"This yer Squawkin' Henry, boss, he's a no-good hound. He's no good a-a-atall. They ketched him at Butte last year ringin' in hawss dice on 'e crap game 'mong friends an' 'ey jus' nachelly sunk his floatin' ribs an' kicked him out on his haid. Thass all they done to him, Mist' Curry. Betteh watch him clost, else he'll steal 'em gol' fillin's outen yo' teeth!"

"You know him, do you, Mose?" asked Old Man Curry.

"Do I knows him!" ejaculated the little negro. "I knows him well 'nough to wish yo' hadn't 'vited him to do his floppin' in yo' tack-room!"

"Ah-hah!" said Old Man Curry reflectively. "Mose, I reckon you never heard what Job said?"

Jockey Moseby Jones heaved a deep sigh.

"Heah it comes again!" he murmured. "No, boss; he said such a many things I kain't seem to keep track of 'em all. Whut he say now?"

"Something about the wise being taken in their own craftiness; I've forgotten the exact words."

"Umph! Sho'lly yo' don't call Squawkin' Henry *wise*?"

"No-o, but he may have wise friends. Somehow I've sort of been expecting this visitor, Mose. You heard him tell about how bad off his mother is. It seems a shame not to accommodate him, when all he wants is a place to sleep —and some information on the side."

"Info'mation, boss?"

"Well, I can't exactly swear to it, Mose, but I think the children of Israel have sent this Henry person among us to spy out the land. That's a trick they learned a long time ago, after they got out of Egypt. Joshua taught it to 'em. Ever since then they don't take any more chances than they can help. They always want to know what the other fellow is doing—and it's a pretty good system at that. Being as things are the way they are, a spy in camp, etcetry, mebbe what hoss talk is done had better be done by me. You *sabe*, Mose?"

"Humph!" sniffed the little jockey. "I got you long ago, boss, lo-ong ago!"

Al Engle, sometimes known as the Sharpshooter, horse owner and recognised head of a small but busy band of turf pirates, was leaving his stable at seven-thirty on a Wednesday evening, intending to proceed by automobile to the brightly lighted district. Sleek, blond, youthful in appearance, without betraying wrinkle or line, Engle's innocent exterior had been his chief dependence in his touting days. He seemed, on the surface, to be everything which he was not.

As he stepped forth from the shadow of the stable awning a hand plucked at his sleeve.

"It's me—Henry," said a voice. "I've got a message for Goldmark—couldn't catch him on the phone."

"Shoot it!" said Engle.

"Tell him that Elisha has gone dead lame—can't hardly rest his foot on the ground."

"That'll do for Sweeney!" said the Sharpshooter. "Elisha worked fine this morning. I clocked him myself."

"But that was this morning," argued Squeaking Henry. "He must have bowed a tendon or something. His left foreleg is in awful shape."

"Are you sure it's Elisha?" demanded Engle.

"Come and see for yourself. You know the horse. Owned him for a few weeks, didn't you? Curry is working on his leg now. You can peek in at the door of the stall and see for yourself. He won't even know you're there."

Together they crossed the dark space under the trees, heading for a thin ribbon of light which streamed from beneath the awning of Curry's barn. Somewhere, close at hand, a piping voice was lifted in song:

> *"On 'e dummy, on 'e dummy line;*
> *Rise an' shine an' pay my fine;*
> *Rise an' shi-i-ine an' pay my fi-i-ine,*
> *Ridin' on 'e dummy, on 'e dummy, dummy line."*

"What's that?" ejaculated Engle, pausing.

"Aw, that's only Curry's little nigger, Mose. He's always singing or whistling or something!"

"I hope he chokes!" said Engle, advancing cautiously.

The stall door was almost closed, but by applying his eye to the crack Engle could see the interior. Old Man Curry was kneeling in the straw, dipping bandages in a bucket of hot water. The horse was watching him, ears pricked nervously.

"If this ain't tough luck, I don't know what is!" Old Man Curry was talking to himself, his voice querulous and complaining. "Tough luck—yes, sir! Tough for you, 'Lisha, and tough for me. Job knew something when he said that man born of woman is of few days and full of trouble. Yes, indeed! Here I had you right on edge, and ready to—whoa, boy! Stand still, there! I ain't goin' to hurt ye, 'Lisha. What's the matter with ye, anyway? *Stand still!*"

The horse backed away on three legs, snorting with indignation. Engle had seen enough. He withdrew swiftly, nor did he pause to chuckle until he was fifty yards from Curry's barn.

"Well," said Squeaking Henry, "it was him, wasn't it?"

"Sure it was him, and he's got a pretty badly strained tendon, too. At first I thought the old fox might be trying to palm off one of his other cripples on you, but that was Elisha all right enough. Yes, he's through for about a month or so."

"That's what I figure," said Henry. "The old man, though, he's got his heart set on starting Elisha in the Handicap next Saturday. He thinks maybe he can dope him up so's he won't feel the soreness."

"In a mile and a half race?" said Engle. "I hope he tries it! He'll just about ruin that skate for life if he does. Five-eighths, yes, but a mile and a half? No chance!"

"You'll tell Goldmark?"

"Yes, I'll tell him. So long."

Engle swung away through the dark and Squeaking Henry watched him until he was swallowed up in the gloom.

"That being the case," said he, "and Elisha on the bum, I guess I'll take a night off. This Sherlock Holmes stuff is wearing on the nerves."

Al Engle delivered the message, giving it a strong backing of personal opinion.

"No, Abe, it's all right, I tell you. It's straight. I've seen the horse myself, ain't I? Know him? Man alive, I had the skate in my barn for nearly a month! I ought to know him. Why, there's no question about it. He's so lame he can hardly touch his foot to the ground. If he starts, he's a million to one to win; a hundred to one he won't even finish. Certainly I'm sure! You can go broke on it. Don't talk to me! Haven't I seen strained tendons before? Next to a broken leg, it's the worst thing that can happen to a race horse."

While Engle was closeted with Goldmark, Old Man Curry was entertaining another nocturnal visitor. It was the Bald-faced Kid, breathless, his brow beaded with perspiration.

"Just got the tip that Elisha has gone lame," said the Kid. "I was in the crap game over at Devlin's barn when Squeaking Henry came in with the news. I ran all the way over here."

"Oho, so it was Henry, eh?" Old Man Curry rumbled behind his whiskers— his nearest approach to a laugh. "Henry, eh? Well, now, it's this way 'bout Henry. He's better than a newspaper because it don't cost a cent to subscribe to him. He's got the loosest jaw and the longest tongue in the world."

"But on the level," said the Kid earnestly, "is Elisha lame?"

"Come and see for yourself," said Old Man Curry, taking his lantern from the peg. After an interval they returned to the tack-room, the Bald-faced Kid shaking his head commiseratingly.

"That would have been rotten luck if it had happened to a dog!" said he. "And the Handicap coming on and all."

"There'll be a better opening price than 3 to 1 now, I reckon," said Old Man Curry grimly.

"Opening price!" ejaculated the Kid, startled. "Say, what are you talking about? You don't mean to tell me you're thinking of starting him with his leg in this shape, old-timer?"

"'M—well, no, not in this shape, exackly."

"But Lordy, man, the Handicap is on Saturday and here it is Wednesday night already. You can't fix up a leg like that in two days. You're going some if you get it straightened out in two weeks. Of course, you can shoot the leg full of cocaine and he'll run on it a little ways, but asking him to go a mile and a half —confound it, old-timer! That's murdering a game horse. You're liable to have a hopeless cripple on your hands when it's over. I tell you, if Elisha was mine——"

"You'd own a real race hoss, son," said Old Man Curry. "Now run along, Frank, and don't try to teach your grandad to suck aigs. I was doctoring hosses before you come to this country at all, and I'm going to doctor this one some more and then go to bed."

Shortly thereafter the good horse Elisha entertained a visitor who brought no lantern with him, but operated in the dark, swiftly and silently. Later a door creaked, there were muffled footfalls under the stable awning and one resounding thump, as it might have been a shod hoof striking a doorsill. Still later Squeaking Henry, returning to his post of duty, saw a light in Elisha's stall and looked in at Old Man Curry applying cold compresses to the left foreleg of a gaunt bay horse with a small splash of white in the centre of the forehead.

"How they coming, uncle?" asked Henry.

"Oh, about the same, I reckon," was the reply.

"You might as well hit the hay. You've been fooling with that leg since dark, but you'll never get the bird ready to fly by Saturday."

"'Wisdom crieth without,'" quoted Old Man Curry sententiously. "'She uttereth her voice in the street.'"

"Quit kidding yourself," argued Henry, "and look how sore he is. You're in big luck if he ain't lame a whole month from now."

"Well," said Old Man Curry, "Solomon says that the righteous man regardeth the life of his beast."

"He does, eh?" Squeaking Henry chuckled unpleasantly. "There's a whole lot of things Solomon didn't know about bowed tendons. That leg needs something besides regards, I'm telling you."

"And I'm listening," said Old Man Curry patiently. "Wisdom will die with you, I reckon, Henry, so take care of yourself."

If the Jungle Circuit knew an event remotely approaching a turf classic, it was the Northwestern Handicap, by usage shortened to "the Handicap." It was their Metropolitan, Suburban, and Brooklyn rolled into one. The winner was crowned with garlands, the jockey was photographed in the floral horseshoe, and the fortunate owner pocketed something more than two thousand dollars —a large sum of money on any race track in the land, but a princely reward to the average jungle owner.

The best horses in training were entered each year and while a scornful Eastern handicapper would doubtless have rated them all among the cheap selling platers, they were still the kings of the jungle tracks, small toads in a smaller puddle, and their annual struggle was anticipated for weeks. Each candidate appeared in the light of a possible winner because the purse was worth trying for and each owner was credited with an honest desire to win. The Handicap was emphatically the "big betting race" of the season.

This year Black Bill, famed for consistent performance and ability to cover a distance of ground, was a pronounced favourite. Black Bill had been running with better horses than the jungle campaigners and winning from them and it was popularly believed that he had been shipped from the South for the express purpose of capturing the Handicap purse. His single start at the meeting had been won in what the turf reporters called "impressive fashion," which is to say that Jockey Grogan brought Black Bill home three lengths in front of his field and but for the strength in his arms the gap would have been a much wider one.

Regulator, a sturdy chestnut, and Miss Amber, a nervous brown mare, were also high in public esteem, rivals for the position of second choice.

"It's a three-horse race," said the wiseacres, "and the others are outclassed. Whatever money there is will be split by Black Bill, Miss Amber, and Regulator. If anything happens to Bill, one of the others will win, but the rest of 'em won't get anything but a hard ride and a lot of dust."

From his position on the block Abe Goldmark looked down on a surging crowd. He was waiting for the official announcement on the third race. The crowd was waiting for the posting of the odds on the Handicap, waiting, money in hand, ready to dash at bargains. Al Engle forced his way through the press and Goldmark bent to listen.

"The old nut is going to start him sure enough," whispered the Sharpshooter. "No—he won't warm him up. Would you throw a gallop into a horse with his leg full of coke? Curry is crazy, but he ain't quite as crazy as that."

"The old boy was putting bandages on him at midnight last night," grinned Goldmark. "Dang it, Al, a man ought to be arrested for starting a horse in that condition."

"The coke will die out before he's gone half a mile," said Engle. "Might not even last that long—depends on how long they're at the post. I saw a horse once——"

The melodious bellow of the official announcer rose above the hum of the crowd and there was a sudden, tense shifting of the nervous human mass. A dozen bookmakers turned leisurely to their slates, a dozen pieces of chalk were poised aggravatingly—and a hoarse grunt of disappointment rose from the watchers. Black Bill the favourite, yes, but bet fives to win threes? Hardly. Wait a minute; don't go after it now. Maybe it'll go up. Regulator, 8 to 5— Holy Moses! What kind of booking is this, anyway? Miss Amber, 2 to 1.

"Make 'em *all* odds on and be done with it!" sneered the gamblers. "Talk about your syndicate books! Beat five races at this track and if your money holds out you may beat the sixth, too. Huh!"

One bookmaker, more adventurous than his fellows, offered 4 to 5 on Black Bill and was immediately mobbed. Then came the prices on the outsiders.

Simple Simon, 8 to 1; Pepper and Salt, 12 to 1; Ted Mitchell and Everhardt, 15 to 1; and so on. Last of all, the chalk paused at Elisha—40 to 1.

"Aw, be game!" taunted Al Engle. "Only 40—with what you know about him? He ought to be 100, 40, and 20! Be game!"

"Who's doing this?" demanded Goldmark. "Come on, gentlemen! Make your bets! We haven't got all day. Black Bill, 6 to 10. Simple Simon, 40 to 5. Thank *you*, sir."

Out in the paddock Old Man Curry rubbed the red flannel bandage on Elisha's leg, stopping now and then to answer questions.

"Eh? Yes, been a little lame. Will he last? Well, it's this way; you can't never tell. If it comes back on him—no, I didn't warm him up. Why not? That's *my* business, young man."

The Bald-faced Kid came also, alert as a fox, eager for any scrap of information which might be converted into coin. He shook his head reprovingly at Old Man Curry.

"I didn't think you'd have the heart, old-timer," said he. "Honest to Pete, I didn't! Don't you care what happens to this horse or what?"

"Son," said the patriarch simply, "I care a lot. I care a-plenty. If you've got any of that seven dollars left, you might put it on his nose."

"Him? To win? You're daffy as a cuckoo bird! Why, last night he couldn't put that foot on the ground!"

"Well, of course, Frank, if you know that much about it, don't let me advise you. If I had seven dollars and was looking for a soft spot I'd put it square on 'Lisha's nose."

"You've been losing too much sleep lately," said the Kid, edging away. "You want to win this race so much that you've bulled yourself into thinking that you can."

"Mebbe so, Frank, mebbe so," was the mild response, "but don't let me influence you none whatever. Go play Black Bill. What's his price?"

"Three to five. One to two in some books."

"False price!" said the old man. "He ain't got no license to be odds on."

"See you later!" said the Bald-faced Kid, and went away with a pitying grin upon his face. The pity was evenly divided between Elisha and his owner.

Old Man Curry heaved little Mose into the saddle.

"Mind now, son. Ride just like I told you. Stay with that black hoss. He'll lay out of it the first mile. When he moves up, you move up too. We've got a big pull in the weights and that'll count in the last quarter. Stay with him, just like his shadow, Mose."

"Yes, suh," said Jockey Jones. "If I'm goin' to be his shadder, he'll sho' think the sun is settin' behind him when he starts down at stretch!"

Abe Goldmark craned his neck to see the parade pass the grand stand. Elisha was fifth in line, walking sedately, as was his habit.

"Not so very frisky, but at that he looks better than I thought he would," was Goldmark's mental comment. "They must have shot all the coke in the world into that old skate. As soon as he begins to run the blood will pump into that sore leg and he'll quit. Black Bill looks like the money to me. He outclasses these other horses."

Goldmark passed the eraser over his slate. Black Bill, 2 to 5. Elisha, 60, 20, and 10.

A dozen restless, high-strung thoroughbreds and a dozen nervous, scheming jockeys can make life exceedingly interesting for an official starter, particularly if the race be an important one and a ragged start certain to draw a storm of adverse criticism. The boys on the front runners were all manœuvring to beat the barrier and thus add to a natural advantage while the boys on the top-weighted horses were striving to secure an early start before the lead pads began to tell on their mounts. As a result the barrier was broken four times in as many minutes and the commandment against profanity was broken much oftener. The starter grew hoarse and inarticulate; sweat streamed down his face as he hurled anathemas at horses and riders.

"Keep that Miss Amber back, Dugan! Go through that barrier again and it'll cost you fifty! —— —— ——!!"

"I can't do nothing with her!" whined Dugan. "She's crazy; that's what she is!"

Through all the turmoil and excitement two horses remained quietly in their positions waiting for the word. These were Black Bill and Elisha, stretch runners, to whom a few yards the worst of the start meant nothing. Out of the corner of his eye little Mose watched Jockey Grogan on the favourite. The black horse edged toward the webbing, the line broke, wheeled, advanced, broke again and a third time came swinging forward. As it advanced, Mose drove the blunt spurs into Elisha's side. A roar from the starter, a spattering rain of clods, a swirl of dust—and the Handicap was on.

"Nice start!" said the presiding judge, drawing a long breath.

Across the track, the official starter mopped his brow.

"Not so worse," said he. "Go on, you little devils! It's up to you!"

Away went the front runners, their riders checking them and rating their speed with an eye to the long journey. Simple Simon, Pepper and Salt, and Ted Mitchell engaged in a brisk struggle for the pace-making position and the latter secured it. Miss Amber and Regulator were in fifth and sixth places respectively, and at the tail end of the procession was Black Bill, taking his time, barely keeping up with the others. A distance race was no new thing to Black Bill. He had seen front runners before and knew that they had a habit of fading in the final quarter. Beside him was Elisha, matching him, stride for stride.

Down the stretch they came, Ted Mitchell gradually increasing the pace. Jockey Jones heard the crowd cheering as he passed the grand stand and his lip curled.

"We eatin' it now, 'Lisha hawss," said he, "but nex' time we come down yere they'll be eatin' *ow'* dust an' don't make no mistake! Take yo' time, baby. It's a long way yit, a lo-ong way!"

Entering the back stretch there was a sudden shifting of the coloured jackets. The outsiders, nervous and overeager, were making their bids for the purse, and making them too soon. The flurry toward the front brought about a momentary spurt in the pace followed immediately by the steady, machine-like advance of Regulator, but as the chestnut horse moved up the brown mare went with him, on even terms.

"There goes Regulator! There he goes!"

"Yes, but he can't shake Miss Amber! She's right there with him! Oh, you Amber!"

"What ails Black Bill? He's a swell favourite, he is! He ain't done a thing yet."

"He always runs that way," said the wise ones. "Wait till he hits the upper turn."

Abe Goldmark, standing on a stool on the lawn, wrinkled his brow in perplexity. "About time for that bird to quit," said he to himself. "He ain't got any license to run a mile with a leg like that!"

Jockey Moseby Jones was also beginning to wonder what ailed Black Bill. Grogan sat the favourite like a statue, apparently unmoved by the gap widening in front of him.

"We kin wait 'long as he kin, baby," said Mose, comfortingly, "but I sut'ny don't crave to see 'em otheh hawsses so far ahead!"

At the end of the mile Black Bill and Elisha were still at the end of the procession. Miss Amber had managed to shove her brown nose in front, with Regulator at her saddle girth. Many an anxious eye was turned on Black Bill; many saw his transformation but none was better prepared for it than Jockey Moseby Jones. He saw the first wrap slide from Grogan's wrists.

"Come on, baby!" yelled Mose, bumping Elisha with his spurs. "Come on! We got a race here afteh all! Yes, suh, 'is black hawss wakin' up! Show him something, baby! Show him ow' *class*!"

Jockey Grogan laughed and flung an insult over his shoulder.

"Class? That skate?" said he. "Stay with us as long as you can. This is a-a-a horse, nigger, a-a-a horse!"

Black Bill was beginning to run at last, as the grand stand acknowledged with frenzied yells. Yes, he was running, but a gaunt bay horse was running with him, stride for stride. Old Man Curry, at the paddock gate, tugged at his beard with one hand and fumbled for his tobacco with the other.

Side by side the black and the bay swept upon the floundering outsiders, overwhelmed them, and passed on. Side by side they turned into the home stretch, and only two horses were in front of them—Regulator and Miss Amber. The mare was under the whip.

"You say you got a-a-a hawss there!" taunted Mose. "Show me how much hawss he is!"

Grogan shook off the last wrap and bent to his work. Not until then did he realise that the real race was beside him and not with the chestnut out in front.

"Show him up, 'Lisha! Show him up!" shrilled Mose, and the bay responded with a lengthened stride which gave him an advantage to be measured in inches, but Black Bill gamely fought his way back on even terms again. Miss Amber dropped behind. The boy on Regulator was using his whip, but he might just as well have been beating a carpet with it. Third money was his at the paddock gate.

Seventy-five yards—fifty yards—twenty-five yards—and still the two heads bobbed side by side. Jockey Michael Grogan, hero of many a hard finish; cool, calculating, and unmoved by the deafening clamour beating down from the packed grand stand, measured the distance with his eye—and took a chance. His rawhide whip whistled through the air. Black Bill, unused to punishment, faltered for the briefest fraction of a second, and came on again, but too late.

The presiding judge, an unprejudiced man with a stubby grey moustache, squinted across an imaginary line and saw the bay head before he saw the black. "*Jee-roozalum, my happy home!*" said he. "That was an awful tight fit, but the Curry horse won—by a whisker. Hang up the numbers. Lord! But that Elisha is a better horse than I gave him credit for being!"

"Yeh," said the associate judge, "and the nigger outrode Grogan, if anybody should ask you. He had a chance—if he hadn't let that horse's head flop to go the bat!"

"It wasn't that," said the other quickly. "The horse flinched when he hit him."

"I been photographed and interviewed till I'm black in the face," complained Old Man Curry, "and now you come along. You're worse than them confounded reporters!"

"You bet I am," was the calm response of the Bald-faced Kid, "because I know more. And yet I don't know enough to satisfy me. Somebody played Elisha, and it wasn't me. You never went near the betting ring. I watched you."

"My money did. Quite a gob of it."

"And you—you thought he'd win?"

"Didn't I tell you to bet on him?"

"Hell!" wailed the Bald-faced Kid. "He was *lame*—he couldn't walk the night before! Bet on him? How could I after I'd seen him in that fix?"

"Frank," said the old man, "you believe everything you see, don't you?"

The Bald-faced Kid sat down and took his head in his hands.

"Tell it to me, old-timer," said he humbly. "I'm such a wise guy that it hurts me; but something has come off here that's a mile over my head. Tell me; I'm no mind reader."

Old Man Curry combed his beard reflectively and gazed through the tack-room door into the dusk of the summer evening.

"Son," said he at length, "you never swapped hosses much, did you?"

"Never owned any to swap," was the muffled response.

"Too bad. You would have learned things. For instance, there's a trick that can be worked when you want to buy a hoss cheap and can get at him for a minute. It's done with a needle and thread and a hair from the hoss's tail. There's a spot in the leg where the tendons come together, and the trick is to pass that hosshair in between the tendons and trim off the ends just long enough so's you can find 'em again. Best part of the trick is it don't hurt the hoss none, but he knows it's there and he won't hardly rest his foot on the ground till it's pulled out. Then he's as good as new again."

"Lovely!" groaned the Kid. "What makes you so close-mouthed, old-timer?"

"Experience, son, experience. 'He that hath knowledge spareth his words.' I spared quite a-many. I knew there was a spy in camp, and I sewed up Elisha on Wednesday and let Henry see him. Al Engle came over and peeked to make sure. I had the little nigger watching for him. You saw Elisha that same night, and the whole kit and boiling of you got a couple of notions fixed in your heads—first, that it *was* Elisha; second, that he was a tol'able lame hoss. You expected, when you looked in that stall again, you'd see a big red hoss with a white spot on his forehead—lame. Well, you did, but it wasn't the same one."

"Elijah!" said the Kid. "And you lamed him too?"

"I had to do it. People expected to see a lame hoss; I had to have one to show 'em, didn't I? But nobody got a look at him in bright daylight, son. After you went away Wednesday night I pulled out the hosshair, put Elisha in Elijah's stall, and vice versey, as they say. Then I worked on Elijah, and when Henry came along he didn't know the difference. Them hosses look a lot alike, anyway; put a little daub of white stuff on Elijah's forehead, keep him blanketed up pretty snug, and—well, I reckon that's about all they was to it."

"Fifty and sixty to one—going begging!" mourning the Kid. "Why didn't you tell me what was coming off?"

"Because Henry was watching both of us," was the reply. "And, speaking of Henry, it was you told me the sons of Belial had gone into the spy business, so I p'tected your interests the best I could. Here's a little ticket calling for quite a mess of money. It's on the Abe Goldmark's book, and I didn't cash it because I wanted you to have a chance to laugh at him when he pays off. Last I seen of him he was sore but solvent."

THE LAST CHANCE

It was the Bald-faced Kid who christened him Little Calamity because, as he explained, Jockey Gillis was a sniffling, whining, half portion of hard luck and a disgrace to the disreputable profession of touting. "Every season," said the Bald-faced Kid, "is a tough season for a guy like that. He carries his hard luck with him. He's cockeyed something awful; his face was put on upside down; you can't tell whether he's looking you in the eye or watching out for a policeman, and drunks shy clear across the betting ring to get away from him. That's the tip-off; when a souse won't listen to your gentle voice, it's time to change your system of approach. This Little Calamity person has only got one thing in his favour, and that's an honest face; he *looks* like a thief, and, by golly, he *is* one. He couldn't sell a twenty-dollar gold piece for a dime or make a sucker put down a bet with the winning numbers already hanging on the board in front of him. They all give him the once over and holler for the police. And as for his riding, he's about as much help to a horse as a fine case of the heaves. I'm darned if I know how he manages to live!"

Little Calamity sometimes wondered about this himself. Of course there were the rare occasions when he was able to persuade a weak-minded owner to give him a mount on a hopeless outsider or a horse entered only for the sake of the workout, but the five-dollar jockey fees were few and far between. They could not be stretched to cover the intervening periods, so Little Calamity did his best to be a petty larcenist with indifferent success.

He infested the betting ring with a persistence almost pitiful, but he had neither the appearance nor the manner which begets confidence in unlikely tales, and in his mouth the truth itself sounded like a fabrication. He was a willing but an unconvincing liar, and the few who lingered long enough to listen to his clumsy attempts went away smiling.

Little Calamity was nearer thirty than twenty, wrinkled and weazened and bow-legged. Worse than everything else, he was cross-eyed. The direct and compelling gaze is an absolute necessity in the touting business because the average man believes that the liar will be unable to look him in the eye. Little Calamity could not look any man in the eye without first undergoing a surgical operation. He had few acquaintances and no friends; he ate when he could slept where he could, and life to him was just a continued hard-luck story.

Imagine, then, the incredulous amazement of the Bald-faced Kid when Old Man Curry informed him that Jockey Gillis had secured steady employment.

"That shrimp?" said the Kid. "Why, if he had the ice-water privilege in hell he'd starve to death!"

"Frank," said the old man, "I wish you wouldn't be so blame keerless with your figures of speech. There won't be any ice water for the wicked, it says in the Book, and, anyway, it ain't a fit subject to joke about. It don't sound pretty."

The Bald-faced Kid took this reproof with a sober countenance, for he respected the old man's principles even if he did not understand them.

"All right, old-timer. I'll take your word for it. Got a steady job, has he? For Heaven's sake, what doing?"

"Running a racing stable for a man named Hopwood."

"Running a stable! What does Calamity know about training horses?"

"A heap more than Hopwood, I reckon, and, anyway, he'll only have one hoss to experiment on. Hopwood was over here this morning, visiting around and getting acquainted, he said. Awful gabby old coot. He's got a grocery store up in Butte, and used to go out to the race track once in a while. Some of those burglars got hold of him and sold him something with four legs and a tail. They told him it was a sure enough race hoss, and now he's down here to make his fortune. Gillis saw him first, I reckon. Hopwood has hired him by the month— and a percentage of what he wins."

At this the Bald-faced Kid laughed long and loud.

"There's one of 'em born every minute," said he, "but I didn't think the supply was big enough to reach as far as Calamity. Didn't you tell this poor nut what he was up against, trying to horn his way into the Jungle Circuit with one lonely lizard and a human jinx to handle him?"

"No-o," said Old Man Curry, "I didn't. What would be the use! You know what Solomon says about that sort of thing, don't you?"

"I do not," answered the Kid promptly, "but I'll be the goat as usual. What does he say?"

"'Answer not a fool according to his folly, lest thou also be like unto him,'" quoted Old Man Curry, "and that's sound advice, my son. When a fool gets an idea crossways in his head, nothing but a cold chisel will get it out again, and, anyway, people don't thank you for pointing out their mistakes. It's human nature to get mad at a man that can prove he knows more than you do. This Hopwood has got it all whittled down to a fine point how he's going to do right well at the racing game, and the best way is to let him try it a while. It'll cost him money to find out that a grocery store is a safer place for him than a race track. 'A whip for the horse, a bridle for the ass, and a rod for the fool's back.' That's Solomon again. Hopwood has got the gad coming to him for sure."

"Ain't that the truth!" exclaimed the Kid. "By the way, did he mention the name of the beetle that's going to do all this heavy work?"

"That's the best joke of all," said Old Man Curry. "Hopwood stables down at the end of the line, where Gilfeather used to be. Go take a look at what they sold him for five hundred dollars."

"I'll do that little thing," said the Kid, rising. "If he's got any dough left, I may want to sell him something myself!"

Little Calamity was in the box stall, industriously grooming a tall, wild-eyed chestnut animal with four white stockings and a blaze, and as he worked he hummed a tune under his breath. The tune stopped when he became aware of a head thrust in at the open door. The Bald-faced Kid glanced at the horse and his jaw dropped.

"Well, by the limping Lazarus!" he ejaculated. "If they haven't gone and slipped him Last Chance! Yes, I'd know that darned old hay hound if he was stuffed and in a museum, and, by golly, that's where he ought to be! Last Chance!"

"What's it *to* you?" growled Little Calamity sullenly. "Can't you mind your own business?"

"Your boss is in big luck," continued the visitor, pleasantly ignoring Calamity's manner. "The worst horse and the worst jock in the world—a prize package for fair! Last Chance! His name ought to be No Chance!"

"Now looka here," whined Calamity, "I never tried to queer anything for you, did I? Live and let live; that's what I say, and let a guy get by if he can. If you was right up against it and had a chance to grab off eating money, you wouldn't want anybody around knocking, would you? On the level?"

He looked up as he finished, and the Bald-faced Kid's heart smote him. Little Calamity's face was thinner than ever, there were hollows under his wandering eyes, and in them the anxious, wistful look of a half-starved cur which has found a bone and fears that it will be taken away from him. It occurred to the Kid that even a rat like Gillis might have feelings—such feelings as may be touched by hunger and physical discomfort. And there was no mistaking the desperate earnestness of his plea.

"Things have been breaking awful tough for me around here," he went on. "Awful tough. You don't know. And then this Hopwood came along. It ain't my fault if the sucker thinks he's got another Roseben, is it? He wanted a trainer and a jockey, and somebody else would have picked him up if I hadn't. It's the first piece of luck I've had this year. All I want is a chance to string with this fellow as long as he lasts and get a piece of change for myself. That ain't hurting you any, is it? He's my only chance to eat regular; don't go scaring him away."

The Kid was about to reply when a short, fat gentleman waddled around the corner of the barn and paused, wheezing, at the door of the stall. A new owners' badge dangled prominently from his buttonhole, and this he fingered from time to time with manifest pride. He peered in at Last Chance and beamed upon the Bald-faced Kid with the utmost friendliness, his thick eyeglasses giving him the appearance of a jovial owl.

"Well," said he heartily, "I see you're looking him over, young man. He's mine; I just bought him, and I think I got him cheap. Pretty fine-looking horse, eh?"

The Kid nodded gravely.

"You bet your life!" said he with emphasis. "Take it from me, he is *some* horse!"

"Some horse is right!" chimed in Little Calamity fervently. "Just wait till I get him in shape, boss, and I'll show you how much horse he is!"

"And that," said the Bald-faced Kid, "is no idle statement."

"Frank," said Old Man Curry, "you're making more of a fool of that Hopwood than the Lord intended him to be, and it's a sin and a shame. Why can't you let him alone?"

"Because he hands me many a laugh," said the Bald-faced Kid, "and laughs are good for what ails me. He is a three-ring circus and concert all by himself, but he doesn't know it, and that's what makes him so good. And innocent? Say, the original Babes in the Wood haven't got a thing on him. If he stays around here these sharpshooters will have his shirt."

"And you're helping them to get it with your lies. First thing you know you'll have him betting on that hoss when he starts, and Last Chance never won a race in his life and never will. He can quit so fast that it looks like he's going the wrong way of the track. Hopwood was around here to-day all swelled up with the stories you've been feeding him. It ain't right, my son, and, what's more, it ain't *honest*. You might just as well pick his pockets and give the money to the bookmakers."

"The bookmakers won't get fat on what they take away from him," was the careless rejoinder. "This fellow has got a groceryman's heart. He can squeeze a dollar until the eagle screams for help, and he never heard of Riley Grannan. If he bets at all it won't be more than a ten-dollar note. Last Chance goes in the second race to-morrow—nonwinners at the meeting—and I'm going down to the stable now to have a conference and give Calamity his riding orders."

"I wash my hands of you," said the old man. "Fun is all right in its place, but fun that hurts somebody else has a way of coming home to roost. Don't forget that, my son."

"Aw, who's going to hurt him?" was the sulky rejoinder. "I'm only helping the chump to buy some of the experience that you spoke about the other day."

"Solomon says——" began Old Man Curry, but the Kid beat a hasty retreat.

"Put him on ice till to-morrow!" he called back over his shoulder. "This is my busy day!"

For a horse that had never won a race, Last Chance made a gay appearance in the paddock. Little Calamity, conscious of his shortcomings as a trainer, had done his best to offset them by extra activities in his capacity as stable hand. The big chestnut had been groomed and polished until his smooth coat shone like satin and blue ribbons were braided in his mane. The other nonwinners were a sorry-looking lot of dogs when compared with Last Chance, and the owner's bosom swelled with proud anticipation.

"Look at the fire in his eye!" said Hopwood to the Bald-faced Kid. "See how lively he is!"

"Uh-huh," said the Kid, who was present in the rôle of adviser. "He seems to be full of pep to-day."

As a matter of fact, Last Chance was nervous. He knew that a trip to the paddock was usually followed by a beating with a rawhide whip and a prodding with blunt spurs, hence the skittishness of his behaviour and the fire in his eye. Given a decent opportunity he would have jumped the fence and gone home to his stall.

When the bell rang Little Calamity came out of the jockeys' room, radiant as a butterfly in his new silks; he had the audacity to wink when he saw the Kid looking at him.

"What do we do now?" demanded Hopwood, all in a flutter. "This is new to me, you know."

"Well," said the Kid, "I'd say it would be a right pious idea to get this fiery steed saddled up, unless Calamity here is figuring on riding him bareback, which I don't think the judges would stand for."

Later it was the Kid who gave Calamity his riding orders. "All right, boy," said he. "Nothing in here to beat but a lot of lizards. Never look back and make every post a winning one. He can tow-rope this field and drag 'em to death!"

"*Pzzt!*" whispered the jockey. "Not so strong with it, not so strong!"

While the horses were on their way to the post the Bald-faced Kid escorted Hopwood to a position in front of the grand stand.

"You want to be handy in case he wins," said the Kid. "You'll have to go down in the ring if he does. It's a selling race and they might try to run him up on you."

"In the ring, eh?" said Hopwood, straightening his collar and plucking at his tie. "Do I look all right?" But the Kid was coughing so hard that he could not answer the question.

"I can't see very far with these glasses," said Hopwood, "and you'll have to tell me about it. Where is he now?"

"At the post," said the Kid. "The starter won't fool away much time with those ... there they go now! Good start."

Hopwood pawed at the Kid's arm.

"I can't see a thing! Where is he? How's he doing?"

"He broke flying and he's right up in front."

"That's good! That's fine!... And now? Where is he now?"

"Still up in front and winging, just winging. It's an exercise gallop for him. How much did you bet?"

Hopwood took off his glasses and fumbled at them with his handkerchief.

"Where is he now?"

"Second, turning for home. He ought to win all by himself. They're choking to death behind him."

"And I didn't bet a cent!" wailed the owner. "But I said he was a good horse, remember?"

"Sure you did, and he ... oh, tough luck! Well, if that ain't a dirty shame!"

"What is it?" chattered Hopwood. "What happened?"

"They bumped him into the fence, I think.... Yes, he's dropping back. And it looked like a cinch for him, too!… I'm afraid he won't get anything this time…. Too bad! Well, that's racing luck for you. It's to be expected in this game. Sometimes you win and sometimes you lose. Good thing you didn't bet."

"I—I suppose so," gulped the unhappy owner. "Well, next time, eh?"

"That's the proper spirit! Keep after 'em!"

Hopwood put on his glasses in time to see the finish of the race. First came four horses, well bunched; after them the stragglers. Last of all a chestnut with four white stockings and a blaze galloped heavily through the dust, snorting his indignation. Last Chance had been hopelessly last all the way in spite of a rawhide tattoo on his flanks.

The Bald-faced Kid, wishing to forestall a conflict of evidence, made it his business to have the first word with the principal witness. He walked beside Little Calamity as that dispirited midget shuffled down the track from the judges' stand, saddle and tackle on his arm. Close behind them was Hopwood, leading the horse.

"Pretty tough luck," said the Kid, "getting bumped in the stretch when you had the race won." Little Calamity stared from under the peak of his cap in blank, uncomprehending amazement.

"Huh?" he grunted. "Bumped?… Aw, quitcha kiddin'!"

"Well," said the Kid, "the boss couldn't see and I was telling him about the race. It looked to me as if they bumped him."

A gleam of intelligence lighted the straying eyes; instantly the jockey took his cue.

"Oh!" said he, loudly, "you mean in the *stretch*! Yeh, he had a swell chance till then—goin' nice, and all, but the bumping took the run out of him. He'll beat the same bunch like breakin' sticks the next time." Then, under his breath: "*You're a pretty good guy after all!*"

"Well," was the ungracious rejoinder, "don't kid yourself that it's on your account."

Since it was his practice never to accept the obvious but to search diligently for the hidden motive behind every deed, good or bad, Little Calamity gave considerable thought to the matter and at last believed that he had arrived at the only possible explanation of the Kid's conduct. "Boss," said he that evening, "did you bet any money to-day?"

"Not a nickel," was the answer.

"Or give anybody any money to bet for you?"

"No."

"Did anybody ask to be your bettin' commissioner?"

"No. Why?"

"Oh, nothing. I just wanted to know."

Before Little Calamity went to sleep that night he reviewed the situation somewhat as follows:

"My dope was wrong, but it's a cinch a hustler like the Kid ain't hangin' around the boss for his *health*.... And he didn't kick in wit' that alibi because he loves *me* any too well.... I can't figure him at all."

If he could have heard a conversation then going on in Old Man Curry's tackle-room, the figuring would have been easier.

"Frank," said the old man, "I had my eye on you to-day. You ain't got designs on that fool's bank roll, have you?"

The Bald-faced Kid blew a cloud of cigarette smoke into the air and watched it float to the rafters before he answered question with question.

"How long have you known me, old-timer?"

"Quite a while, my son."

"You know that I get my living by doing the best I can?"

"Yes."

"Did you ever know me to steal anything from a blind man? Or even one that was near-sighted?"

"No-o."

"Then don't worry about this Hopwood."

"But he ain't blind—except in the Scriptural sense."

"Think not, eh? Listen! That bird can't see as far as the sixteenth pole. Somebody has got to watch the races and tell him how well his horse is going or else he'll never know. Think what he'd miss! I'm his form chart and his eyes, old-timer, and all I charge him is a laugh now and then. Cheap enough, ain't it?"

Old Man Curry found his packet of fine-cut and thrust a large helping into his left cheek. "'For as the crackling of thorns under a pot,'" he quoted, "'so is the laughter of a fool.'"

The end of the meeting was close at hand; the next town on the Jungle Circuit was preparing to receive the survivors. The owners were plotting to secure that elusive commodity known as get-away money; some of them wouldhave been glad to mortgage their chances for a receipted feed bill. Last Chancehad started five times and each time Hopwood had listened to a thrilling description of the race; the chestnut's performances had been bad enough to strain the Kid's powers of invention.

On the eve of the final struggle of the nonwinners, the Kid sat in grave consultation with Hopwood and Little Calamity and the rain drummed on the shingle roof of the tackle room. The fat man was downcast; he had been hinting about selling Last Chance at auction and returning to Butte.

"You don't mean to say that you're going to *quit*?" demanded the Kid, incredulously. "Just when he's getting good?"

"What's the use?" was the dreary reply. "Luck is against me, ain't it?"

"But he's always knocking at the door, ain't he? He's always right up there part of the way. You can't get the worst of it every time, you know. Be game."

"I've had the worst of it every time so far," said Hopwood, with a dejected shake of his head. "Every time. I swear I don't know what's wrong with that horse. He *looks* all right and he *acts* all right, but every time he starts something happens. They bump him into the fence or pocket him or he gets a clod in his eye and quits. He's been last every time but one and then he was next to last. I—I'm sort of discouraged, boys."

"Aw, never mind, boss!" chirped Little Calamity, one eye on the Kid and the other wandering in the general direction of the owner. "To-morrow is another day and there ain't a thing left in the nonwinner class for him to beat. All the good ones are gone. He worked fine this morning, and——"

"You've said that every time."

"Yes, but you're overlooking the muddy track!" Hopwood blinked in perplexity as the Kid came to the rescue with a new story.

"The muddy track? What difference will that make?"

"Listen to him! All the difference in the wide world!"

"Yeh," chimed in Calamity. "You bet it makes adifference!"

"You're forgetting that Last Chance is by a mudder out of a mudder," suavely explained the Kid. "His daddy used to win stakes kneedeep in it. His mother liked mud so well they had to mix it with her oats to get her to eat regular. What difference will it make? Huh! Wait and see!"

The owner rose, grunting heavily.

"I hope you're right this time," said he. "Lord knows I've had disappointments enough. When I bought this horse they guaranteed him to win at least every other time he started——"

"With an even break in the luck, of course," interrupted the Kid. "You've got to have luck too."

"They didn't mention anything about luck when they took my money." Hopwood was positive on this point. "They told me it was a sure thing and I wouldn't be in this mess if I hadn't thought it was…. You boys talk it over between you. I'm going to ask Mr. Curry if he wants to buy a horse. He can have him for half what he cost me."

Hopwood turned up his collar and departed; the two conspirators listened until his footsteps died away down the row of stables. "Will Curry split on us?" asked Little Calamity, anxiously.

"Not in a thousand years!" was the confident reply. "The old man is a sport in his way. It's a queer way, but he's all right at that. He plays his own string and lets you play yours. Hopwood will find out what Solomon says about buying strange horses, but the old man won't tip your hand or mine. Queer genius, Curry is…. Well, your sucker has lasted longer than I thought he would."

"And now he's getting onto himself," said Calamity mournfully.

"He's not. He's getting cold feet."

"To-morrow is the last crack we'll get at him…. *Can* this beagle run in the mud?"

"How do I know? I was only stringing him."

Little Calamity sighed and the Kid rose to take his departure.

"Wait a minute!" said the other. "Don't go yet. Maybe this horse *will* do better in the mud. You don't know and I don't know, but he *might*."

"What he might do ain't worrying me," said the Kid.

"Listen a second. Maybe you won't believe it, but I've been on the up and up with the boss. Honest, I have. I could have tipped one of the other hustlers to tout him and sink the money for a split, but—well, I didn't do it, that's all. He was white to me and I tried to be white too, see? I even told him not to bet on the horse until I gave him the office, and so far we've been running for nothing but the purse. You haven't touted him either——"

"Draw your bat and make a quick finish!" said the Kid shortly. "What's it all about?"

"Suppose I should talk him into putting a bet down to-morrow?"

"A bet on what?"

"On Last Chance. It ain't no crime for a man to bet on his own horse, is it? He told me he'd give me a percentage of what he won. Maybe the old crowbait will go better in the mud, and I'll ride him until his eyes stick out a foot. We might accidentally get down there to the judges' stand in front, and——"

"And still you haven't said anything," interrupted the Kid. "You want something; what is it?"

"I want you not to queer the play. Hopwood won't bet much; like as not he won't bet anything without putting it up to you first. It's my last chance to pick up a piece of change——"

"Last chance on Last Chance," mused the Kid, "and that's a hunch, but I wouldn't play it with counterfeit Confederate money."

"But if he comes to you, you won't knock it, will you?"

"I'll tell him that as an owner he ought to use his own judgment. If he wants to bet, I'll see that he gets the top price."

"You *are* a good guy!" said Little Calamity. "I think Last Chance will be a better horse to-morrow—somehow."

The Bald-faced Kid shot a keen glance at the jockey.

"What do you mean, a better horse? A powder on his tongue, maybe?"

Calamity shook his head.

"I never hopped a horse; I wouldn't know how to go about it. If I got to fooling with them speed powders I might give him too much and have him climbing a tree on the way to the post.... Cheese it! Here comes the boss!"

Hopwood entered, shaking the water from the brim of his hat, his lower lip sagging and an angry light in his eye.

"Well," asked the Kid from the doorway, "what did Curry say?"

"Umph!" grunted the fat man, disgustedly. "He read me a chapter out of Proverbs. It was all about the difference between a wise man and a fool. Confound it! He needn't have rubbed it in!"

It was the last race of the day and from their sheltered pagoda the judges looked out upon the river of mud which had been the home stretch. Forty- eight hours of rain had turned it into a grand canal. The presiding judge scowled as he examined the opening odds. "Nonwinners, eh? Same old bunch of hounds. Grayling, 2 to 1; Ivy Leaf, 4 to 1; Montezuma, 10 to 1; Bluestone,

10 to 1; Alibi, 15 to 1; Stuffy Eaton, 25 to 1—and here's Last Chance again! I wonder where Hopwood got that horse? Remember him, two years ago at Butte? I thought he was pulling a junk wagon by now. Last Chance, 50 to 1. Jockey Gillis; hm-m-m. There's a sweet combination for you! A horse that can't untrack himself, a jockey that never rode a winner, and a half-witted grocer! Why couldn't the chump stick to the little villainies that he knows about—sanding the sugar and watering the kerosene? I declare, sir, if I had half an excuse I'd refuse the entry of that horse and warn Hopwood away from here! It would be an act of Christian charity to do it."

The Bald-faced Kid, faithful to the bitter end, assisted in the paddock as usual. Last Chance, his tail braided in a hard knot and minus the ribbons in his mane, submitted to the saddling process with unusual docility. His customary attitude of protest seemed to be swallowed up in a gloomy acquiescence to fate. It was as if he said: "You can do this to me again if you want to, but I assure you now that it is useless, quite useless."

Calamity leaned down from the saddle and whispered in the Kid's ear:

"You can get 50 and 60 to 1 on him! The boss said he'd make a bet. Don't let him overlook it!"

When the bugle sounded, Hopwood grasped the bridle and led the horse through the chute to the track. The rain beat hard upon his hunched shoulders and his feet plowed heavily through the puddles. Repeated failure had robbed him of the pride of ownership and all confidence in horseflesh. He was, as the Bald-faced Kid said to himself, "a sad looking mess." Hopwood spoke but once, wasting no words.

"Make good if you're going to," said he tersely, "because win or lose I'm *through*!"

"Yes, boss, and don't forget what I told you. To-day's the day to bet on him. Go to it!"

Last Chance splashed away down the track and Hopwood turned on his heel with a growl.

"Come along!" said he to the Kid. "I might as well be all the different kinds of fool while I'm about it!"

"Where to now?" asked the Kid innocently.

"To the betting ring," was the grim response. "I said I'd bet on him this time and I will! Come along!"

From his perch on the inside rail the official starter eyed the nonwinners with undisguised malevolence. Some of them were cantering steadily toward the barrier, some were walking and one, a black brute, seemed almost unmanageable, advancing in a series of wild plunges and sudden sidesteps.

"Ah, hah," said the starter, with suitable profanity. "Old Alibi has got his hop in him again! I'll recommend the judges to refuse his entry." Then, to his assistant: "Jake, take hold of that crazy black thing and lead him up here. Don't let go of his head for a second or he'll be all over the place! Lively now! I want to get out of this rain…. Walk 'em up, you crook-legged little devils! *Walk 'em up, I say!*"

Last Chance advanced sedately to his position, which was on the outer rail. Grayling, the favourite, had drawn the inner rail. Jake, obeying orders, swung his weight on Alibi's bit and dragged the rearing, plunging creature into the middle of the line. At that instant the starter jerked the trigger and yelled:

"Come on! Come on!"

The whole thing happened in the flicker of an eyelid. As Jake released his hold, Alibi whirled at right angles and bolted for the inner rail, carrying Grayling, Ivy Leaf, Satsuma, and Jolson with him. They crashed into the fence, a squealing, kicking tangle, above which rose the shrill, frightened yells of the jockeys. This left but four horses in the race, and one of them, old Last Chance, passed under the barrier with a wild bound which all but unseated his rider. It was not his habit to display such unseemly haste in getting away from the post and, to do him justice, Last Chance was no less surprised—and shocked—than a certain young man of our acquaintance.

"Well, look at that lizard go!" gasped the Bald-faced Kid. *"Look—at—him—go!"*

"Honest Injun?" asked Hopwood. "Is he going—really?"

"Is he going! He's going crazy! And listen to this! That black thing carried a big bunch of 'em into the fence and they're out of it! Only four in the race and we're away flying! Do you get that? Flying!"

"Honest?"

"Can't you hear the crowd hissing the rotten start?"

"Well," said Hopwood, "it—it's about time I had a little luck."

"That skate has got something besides luck with him to-day!" exclaimed the Kid. "I wonder now—did he try a powder after all? But no, he was quiet enough on the way to the post."

Seeing nothing ahead of him but mud and water, Jockey Gillis steered Last Chance toward the inner rail.

"Don't you quit on me, you crab!" he muttered. "Don't you quit! Keep goin' if you don't want me to put the bee on you again! Hi-ya!"

Montezuma, Bluestone, and Stuffy Eaton were the other survivors—bad horses all. Their riders, realizing that something had happened to the real contenders, drove them hard and on the upper turn Jockey Gillis, peering over his shoulder, saw that he was about to have competition. He began to boot Last Chance in the ribs, but the aged chestnut refused to respond to such ordinary treatment.

"All right!" said Jockey Gillis, savagely. "If you won't run for the spurs, you'll run for *this*!" And he drove his clenched fist against the horse's shoulder. Last Chance grunted and did his best to leap out from under his tormentor. Failing in this he spurted crazily and the gap widened.

"There it goes again!" muttered the Kid, under his breath. "He's pretty raw with it. Now if the judges notice the way that horse is running they may frisk Calamity for an electric battery and if they find one on him—good night!"

"Where is he now?" demanded Hopwood.

"Still in front—if he can stay there."

"Honest—is he?"

"*Ask* anybody!" howled the Kid, in sudden anger. "You don't need to take my word for it!"

At the paddock gate Last Chance was rocking from side to side with weariness and the pursuit was closing in on him. Jockey Gillis measured the distance to the wire and waited until Montezuma and Bluestone drew alongside. Twenty-five feet from home his fist thumped Last Chance on the shoulder again. The big chestnut answered with a frenzied bound and came floundering under the wire, a winner by a neck.

"He won!" cried Hopwood. "That—that was him in front, wasn't it?"

"That was what's left of him," was the response. "Maybe we'd better not cheer until the judges give us the 'official' on those numbers. I've got a hunch they may want to see Jock Gillis in the stand." And to himself: "The fool! He handed it to him again right under their noses! Does he think the judges are cockeyed too?"

"Here's our chance to get rid of the grocer," said the presiding judge to his associate. "Did you notice the way that horse acted? The boy's got a battery on him, sure as guns!"

One hundred yards from the wire Last Chance checked to a walk and as Jockey Gillis turned the horse he tossed a small, dark object over the inside fence. It fell in a puddle of water and disappeared from sight. When the winner staggered stiffly into the ring, Gillis flicked the visor of his cap with his whip.

"Judges?" he piped.

The presiding judge answered the salute with a nod, but later when the rider was leaving the weighing room, he halted him with a curt command.

"Bring that tack up here, boy!"

The investigation, while brief, was thorough. The judges examined the saddle carefully for copper stitching, looked at the butt end of the whip, ran their hands over Calamity's thin loins and last of all felt in his bootlegs for wires connected with the spurs. All this time Jockey Gillis might have been posing as a statue of outraged innocence.

"Nothing on him," said the presiding judge shortly. "Hang up the official."

Jockey Gillis bowed and saluted.

"Judges, can I go now?" said he.

"Yes," said the presiding judge, "and don't come back. You're warned off, understand?"

"Judges," whined Jockey Gillis, "I ain't done a thing wrong. That old horse, he——"

"Git!" said the presiding judge. "Now where is that man Hopwood? If he bet much money on this race——"

The Bald-faced Kid was waiting at the paddock gate. He greeted Little Calamity with blistering sarcasm.

"You're a sweet little boy, ain't you? A *nice* little boy! Here I stall for you for weeks and you didn't even tell me that the old skate was going to have the Thomas A. Edison trimmings with him to-day!"

"Honest," said the jockey, "I didn't think there was enough 'lectricity in the world to make it a cinch. I took a long chance myself, that's all. I had to do it."

"And got caught with the battery on you, too. Didn't you know any better'n to slip him the juice right in front of the wire? Think those judges are blind?"

"Well," said Little Calamity, "I don't know how good their eyes are, at that. Jock Hennessey, he's been riding with a hand buzzer every time the stable checks are down. This morning he loaned it to me."

"Oh, it was a hand buzzer, eh?"

"Sure. I chucked it over the fence when I was turning him around after the race."

"Fine work. What did the judges say to you?"

"They warned me away from the track. I should worry. There's other tracks. Only thing is, they've got Hopwood in the stand now, and he'll be fool enough to tell 'em this was the first time he bet on the horse. Somehow, I'd hate to see the old bird get into trouble.... Say, by the way, how much did he bet?"

The Bald-faced Kid began to laugh. He laughed until he had to lean on the rail for support.

"Don't worry," said he, at last. "The judges won't be too hard on him. He hunted all over the ring until he found some 75 to 1 and then he bet the wad—two great big iron dobey dollars—all at once, mind you!"

"Two dollars!" gasped Little Calamity. "*Two dollars?*"

"It serves you right for not letting me know about the buzzer! I'd have made him bet more. As it stands, your cut will be seventy-five—if he splits with you, and I think he will. That's a lot of money—when you haven't got it."

"Bah! Chicken feed!" This with an almost lordly scorn. "It's a good thing those judges didn't take off my boots. Then they *would* have found something!" He fumbled for a moment and produced eight pasteboards. "I had sixteen dollars saved up and one of the boys bet it for me—every nickel of it on the nose. Seventy-five dollars! I'm over eight hundred winner to the race!"

"Holy mackerel!" ejaculated the Kid. "What are you going to do with all that money?"

"I'm goin' to buy a diamond pin and a gold watch and a ring with a red stone in it and a suit of clothes and an overcoat and a derby hat and a pair of silk socks and a porterhouse steak four inches thick and a——"

"E—nough!" said the Kid. "Sufficient! If there's anything left over, you better erect a monument to the guy that discovered electricity!"

This happened long ago. Hopwood's grocery store still does a flourishing business. Over the cash register hangs a crayon portrait of a large yellow horse with four white stockings and a blaze. The original of the portrait hauls the Hopwood delivery wagon. Irritated teamsters sometimes ask Mr. Hopwood's delivery man why he does not drive where he is looking.

SANGUINARY JEREMIAH

It was not yet dawn, but Old Man Curry was abroad; more than that, he was fully dressed. It was a tradition of the Jungle Circuit that he had never been seen in any other condition. The owner of the "Bible horses," in shirt sleeves and bareheaded, would have created a sensation among his competing brethren, some of whom pretended to believe that the patriarch slept in his clothes. Others, not so positive on this point, averred that Old Man Curry slept with one eye open and one ear cocked toward the O'Connor barn, where his enemies met to plot against him.

Summer and winter, heat and cold, there was never a change in the old man's raiment. The rusty frock coat—black where it was not green, grey along the seams, and ravelled at the skirts—the broad-brimmed and battered slouch hat, and the frayed string tie had seen fat years and lean years on all the tracks of the Jungle Circuit, and no man could say when these things had been new or their wearer had been young. Old Man Curry was a fixture, as familiar a sight as the fence about the track, and his shabby attire was as much a part of his quaint personality as his habit of quoting the wise men of the Old Testament and borrowing the names of the prophets for his horses.

The first faint golden glow appeared in the east; the adjoining stables loomed dark in the half light; here and there lanterns moved, and close at hand rose the wail of a sleepy exercise boy, roused from slumber by a liberal application of rawhide. From the direction of the track came the muffled beat of hoofs, swelling to a crescendo, and diminishing to a thin tattoo as the thoroughbreds rounded the upper turn.

Old Man Curry squared his shoulders, turned his face toward the east, and saluted the dawn in characteristic fashion.

"'A time to get and a time to lose; a time to keep and a time to cast away,'" he quoted. "Solomon was framin' up a system for hossmen, I reckon. 'A time to get and a time to lose.' Only thing is, Solomon himself couldn't figure which was which with some of these rascals! *Oh, Mose!*"

"Yessuh, boss! Comin'!"

Jockey Moseby Jones emerged from the tackle-room, rubbing his eyes with one hand and tugging at his sweater with the other. Later in the day he would be a butterfly of fashion and an offence to the eye in loud checks and conflicting colours; now he was only a very sleepy little darky in a dingy red sweater and disreputable trousers.

"Seem like to me I ain't had no sleep a-a-a-tall," complained Mose, swallowing a tremendous yawn. "This yer night work sutny got me goin' south for fair."

Shanghai, the hostler, appeared leading Elisha, the star of the Curry barn.

"Send him the full distance, Mose," said the aged owner, "and set him down hard for the half-mile pole home."

"*Hard*, boss?"

"As hard as he can go."

"But, boss——" There was a note of strong protest in the jockey's voice.

"You heard me," said Old Man Curry, already striding in the direction of the track. "Extend him and let's see what he's got."

"Extend him so's *eve'ybody* kin see whut he's got!" mumbled Mose rebelliously. "Huh!"

In the shadow of the paddock Old Man Curry came upon his friend, the Bald-faced Kid, a youth of many failings, frankly confessed. The Kid sat upon the fence, nursing an old-fashioned silver stop watch, for he was "clocking" the morning workouts.

"Morning, Frank," said Old Man Curry. "You're early."

"But not early enough for some of these birds," responded the Kid. "You galloping something, old-timer?"

"'Lisha'll work in a minute or two."

"Uh-huh. I kind of figured you'd throw another work into him before to-morrow's race. Confound it! If I didn't know you pretty well, I'd say you ought to have your head examined! I'd say they ought to crawl your cupola for loose shingles!"

"And if you didn't know me at all, Frank, you'd say I was just plain crazy, eh?" Old Man Curry regarded his young friend with thoughtful gravity. Here were two wise men of the turf approaching truth from widely varying standpoints, yet able to meet on common ground and exchange convictions to mutual profit. "Spit it out, son," said Old Man Curry. "I'd sort of like to know how crazy I am."

"Fair enough!" said the Bald-faced Kid. "Elisha's a good horse—a cracking good horse—but to-morrow's the end of the meeting and you've gone and saved him up to slip him into the toughest race on the card—on a day when all the burglars at the track will be levelling for the get-away money! You could have found a softer spot for him to pick up a purse, and, take it from me, the winner's end is about all you'll get around here. The bookmakers lost a lot of confidence in human nature when you pulled that horsehair stunt on 'em, and they wouldn't give you a price now, not even if you started a nice motherly old cow against stake horses. As for Elisha—the bookies begin reaching for the erasers the minute they hear his name! You couldn't bet 'em diamonds against doughnuts on that horse. They've been stung too often."

"Maybe I wasn't aiming to bet on him," was the mild reply.

"Then why put him up against such a hard game?"

"Oh, it was a kind of a notion I had. I know it'll be a tough race. Engle is in there, and O'Connor and a lot more that have been under cover. 'Lisha is goin' a mile this morning. Better catch him when he breaks. He's off!"

Whatever Jockey Moseby Jones thought of his orders, he knew better than to disobey them. He sent Elisha the distance, driving him hard from the half- mile pole to the wire, and the Bald-faced Kid's astounded comments furnished a profane obbligato.

"Take a look at that!" said he, thrusting the watch under Old Man Curry's nose. "Pretty close to the track record for a mile, ain't it? And every clocker on the track got him too! If I was you I'd peel the hide off that nigger for showing a horse up like that!"

"No-o," said Old Man Curry, "I reckon I won't lick Mose—this time. You forgot that Jeremiah is goin' in the last race to-morrow, didn't you?"

"Jeremiah!" The Bald-faced Kid spoke with scorn. "Why, he bleeds every time out! It's a shame to start him!"

"Maybe he won't bleed to-morrow, Frank."

"He won't, eh?" The Bald-faced Kid drew out the leather-backed volume which was his constant companion, and began to thumb the leaves rapidly. "You're always heaving your friend Solomon at me. I'll give you a quotation I got out of the Fourth Reader at school—something about judging the future by the past. Look here: *'Jeremiah bled and was pulled up.'* *'Jeremiah bled badly.'* Why, everybody around here knows that he's a bleeder!"

"There you go again," said Old Man Curry patiently. "You study them dad-burned dope sheets, and all you can see is what a hoss *has* done. You listen to me: it ain't what a hoss did last week or last month—it's what he's goin' to do to-day that counts."

"A quitter will quit and a bleeder will bleed," said the Kid sententiously.

"And Jeremiah says the leopard can't change his spots," said Old Man Curry. "Have it your own way, Frank."

Exactly twenty-four hours later the Bald-faced Kid, peering across the track to the back stretch, saw Old Man Curry lead a black horse to the quarter pole, exchange a few words with Mose, adjust the bit, and stand aside.

"What's that one, Kid?" The question was asked by Shine McManus, a professional clocker employed by a bookmaker to time the various workouts and make a report on them at noon.

"That's Jeremiah," said the Kid. "The old man hasn't worked him much lately."

"Good reason why," said Shine. "I wouldn't work a horse either if he bled every time he got out of a walk! There he goes!"

Jeremiah went to the half pole like the wind, slacked somewhat on the upper turn, and floundered heavily into the stretch.

"Bleeding, ain't he?" asked Shine.

"He acts like it—yes, you can see it now."

As Jeremiah neared the paddock he stopped to a choppy gallop, and the railbirds saw that blood was streaming from both nostrils and trickling from his mouth.

"Ain't that sickening? You wouldn't think that Old Man Curry would abuse a horse like that!"

The Bald-faced Kid went valiantly to the defence of his aged friend. He would criticise Old Man Curry if he saw fit, but no one else had that privilege.

"Aw, where do you get that abusing-a-horse stuff! It don't really *hurt* a horse any more'n it would hurt you to have a good nosebleed. It just chokes him up so't he can't get his breath, and he quits, that's all."

"Yes, but it looks bad, and it's a shame to start a horse in that condition."

The argument waxed long and loud, and in the end the Kid was vanquished, borne down by superior numbers. The popular verdict was that Old Man Curry ought to be ashamed of himself for owning and starting a confirmed bleeder like Jeremiah.

On get-away day the speculative soul whose financial operations show a loss makes a determined effort to plunge a red-ink balance into a black one. On get-away day the honest owner has doubts and the dishonest owner has fears. On get-away day the bookmaker wears deep creases in his brow, for few horses are "laid up" with him, and he wonders which dead one will come to life. On get-away day the tout redoubles his activities, hoping to be far away before his victims awake to a sense of injury. On get-away day the program boy bawls his loudest and the hot-dog purveyor pushes his fragrant wares with the utmost energy. On get-away day the judges are more than usually alert, scenting outward indications of a "job." On get-away day the betting ring boils and seethes and bubbles; the prices are short and arguments are long; strange stories are current and disquieting rumours hang in the very air.

"Now, if ever!" is the motto.

"Shoot 'em in the back and run!" is the spirit of the day, reduced to words.

In the midst of all this feverish excitement, Old Man Curry maintained his customary calm. He had seen many get-away days on many tracks. Elisha was entered in the fourth race, the feature event of the day, and promptly on the dot, Elisha appeared in the paddock, steaming after a brisk gallop down the stretch.

Soon there came a wild rush from the betting ring; the prices were up and Elisha ruled the opening favourite at 7 to 5. Did Mr. Curry think that Elisha could win? Wasn't the price a little short? In case Mr. Curry had any doubts about Elisha, what other horse did he favour? The old man answered all questions patiently, courteously, and truthfully—and patience, courtesy, and truth seldom meet in the paddock.

We-ell, about 'Lisha, now, he was an honest hoss and he would try as hard to win at 7 to 5 as any other price. 'Lisha was trained not to look in the bettin' ring on the way to the post. Ye-es, 'Lisha had a chance; he always had a chance 'count of bein' honest and doin' the best he knowed how. The other owners? Well, now, it was this way: he couldn't really say what they was up to; he expected, though, they'd all be tryin'. Himself person'ly, he only bothered about his own hosses; they kept his hands full. Was Engle going to bet on Cornflower? Well, about Engle—hm-m-m. He's right over there, sonny; better ask him.

After Little Mose had been given his riding orders—briefly, they were to do the best he could and come home in front if possible—Old Man Curry turned Elisha over to Shanghai and went into the betting ring. Elisha's price was still 7 to 5. The old man paused in front of the first book, a thick wallet in his fingers. The bookmaker, a red-eyed, dyspeptic-looking person, glanced down, recognised the flowing white beard under the slouch hat, took note of the thick wallet, and with one swipe of his eraser sent Elisha to even money.

"That's it! Squawk before you're hurt!" grunted Elisha's owner, shouldering his way through the crowd to the next stand.

This bookmaker was an immensely fat gentleman with purplish jowls and piggy eyes which narrowed to slits as they rested upon the corpulent roll of bills which Old Man Curry was holding up to him.

"Don't want it," he wheezed.

"What ails it?" Old Man Curry's voice rose in a high, piping treble, shrill with wrath. "It's good money. I got some of it from you. Your slate says 6 to 5, 'Lisha."

"Don't want it," repeated the bookmaker, his eyes roving over the crowd. "Get it next door."

"That's a fine howdy-do!" snapped the exasperated old man. "I can't bet on my own horse—at a short price, too!"

Word ran around the betting ring that Old Man Curry was trying to bet so much money on Elisha that the bookmakers refused his wagers, and there was an immediate stampede for the betting booths and a demand for Elisha at any figure.

The third bookmaker forestalled all argument by wiping out the prophet's price entirely, while the crowd jeered.

"Does a bet scare you that bad?" asked Old Man Curry with sarcasm.

"Any bet from you would scare me, professor. Any bet at all. Try the next store."

Old Man Curry worked his way around the circle, Elisha's price dropping before his advance. His very appearance in the ring had been enough to encourage play on the horse, and the large roll of bills which he carried so conspicuously added a powerful impetus to the rush on the favourite.

"Curry's betting a million!"

"Elisha's a cinch!"

"The old coot's got 'em scared!"

Elisha dropped to even money, then went to odds on. At 4 to 5 and even at 3 to 5 the crowd played him, and sheet and ticket writers were kept busy recording bets on the Curry horse.

Somewhere in the maelstrom Old Man Curry encountered the Bald-faced Kid plying his vocation. He was earnestly endeavouring to persuade a whiskered rustic to bet more money than he owned on Cornflower at 3 to 1. Though very busy, the young man was abreast of the situation and fully informed of events, as indeed he usually was. Retaining his interest in the rustic by the simple expedient of thrusting a forefinger through his buttonhole, the Kid leaned toward the old man.

"See what your little nigger did, riding that horse out yesterday morning? You might have got 2 or 3 to 1 on him if Mose hadn't tipped him off to every clocker at the track!"

Old Man Curry digested this remark in silence.

"I hear that Engle is sending the mare for a killing," whispered the Kid. "Know anything about it?"

"Everything is bein' sent for a killing to-day," said Old Man Curry. "Well, she'll have 'Lisha to beat, I reckon. And all he's runnin' for is the purse, Frank, like you said. I did my best to bet 'em until the price got too plumb ridiculous, but the children of Israel wouldn't take my money."

The Bald-faced Kid glanced at the roll of bills which the old man still held in his hand.

"Well, no wonder!" he snorted. "Don't you know that ain't any way to do? You come in here and wave a chunk like that under their noses, and—by golly, you ought to have your head examined!"

"I reckon you're right," said the old man apologetically. "All I ask is please don't have me yanked up before the Lunacy Board till after the last race, because——"

"Aw, rats! Beat it now till I land this sucker!"

"Frank," whispered the old man, "tell him to save a couple of dollars to bet on Jeremiah!"

It was a great race. Cornflower, lightly weighted, able to set a pace or hold one, did not show in front until the homestretch was reached. Then the mare suddenly shot out of the ruck and flashed into the lead. But she soon had company. Honest old Elisha had been plugging along in the dust for the first half mile, but at that point he began to run, and the Curry colours moved up with great celerity. Merritt, glancing over his shoulders, shook out the last wrap on the mare just as Elisha thundered into second place. Gathering speed with every awkward bound, the big bay horse slowly closed the gap. At the paddock there was no longer daylight between them, and Old Man Curry stopped combing his beard. He knew what that meant. So did Jockey Merritt, plying whip and spur. So did Al Engle and those who had been given the quiet tip to play Cornflower for a killing. So did the Bald-faced Kid, edging away from the rustic who, with a Cornflower ticket clutched in his sweating palm, seemed to be trying to swallow the thyroid cartilage of his larynx. So did Jockey Moseby Jones, driving straight into the hurricane of cheers which beat down from the packed grand stand.

"Elisha! Elisha! Come on, you Elisha!"

Now the gaunt bay head was at the mare's flank, now at the saddle girth, now it blotted out the shoulder, now they were neck and neck; one more terrific bound, an ear-splitting yell from the grand stand, and Elisha's number went slowly to the top of the pole.

The judges were examining the opening betting on the last race of the meeting.

"Ah, we have Old Man Curry with us again!" said the presiding judge. "Jeremiah. If the meeting had another two weeks to run I'd ask him not to start that horse again. I'm told he bled at his workout this morning. By the way, the old man acted sort of grouchy after the Elisha race. Did you notice it?"

"Yes, and I know why," said the associate judge. "He tried to bet a barrel of money and the bookmakers laughed at him. As a general thing he bets a few dollars in each book; this time he went at 'em too strong. The bookies are a little leary of that innocent old boy."

"Call him innocent if you want to. He's either the shrewdest horseman on this circuit—or the luckiest, and I be damned if I can tell which! Hm-m-m. Jeremiah, 20 to 1. If he bled this morning, he ought to be a thousand!"

So, also, thought the employer of Shine McManus, none other than the fat gentleman with the purple jowls, otherwise Izzy Marx, known to his friends as "Easy Marks." McManus was a not unimportant cog in the secret-service department maintained by the bookmaker.

"Listen, Mac!" wheezed Marx. "I want you to tail Old Man Curry from now until the barrier goes up, understand? Yes, yes, you *told* me the horse bled this morning, but that old fox has got the miracle habit; I'd hate to give him too long a price on a *dead* horse, understand, Mac? If Curry is going to bet a plugged nickel on this here Jeremiah, I'll hold him out and not take a cent on him. Stick around close and shoot me back word by Abie. The rest of these fellows have got 20 to 1 on him; he's 15 to 1 in this book until I hear from you. Hurry, now!"

There were ten horses entered in the final race of the meeting, and nine of them were strongly touted as "good things." The tenth was Jeremiah and the most reckless hustler at the track refused to consider the black horse as a contender for anything but sanguinary honours.

"Him? Nix! Didn't you hear about him? Why, he bled this morning in his workout! No chance!"

Of course there were those who did not believe this, so they asked Jeremiah's owner and Old Man Curry stamped up and down the paddock stall and complained querulously. They asked him if Jeremiah had a chance and he replied that Elisha was a good hoss, a crackin' good hoss, but they wouldn't let him bet his money. They asked him if Jeremiah was likely to bleed and he told them that a bookmaker who wouldn't take a bet when it was shoved under his nose ought to be run off the track. They asked him what the other owners were doing and were informed that he had a tarnation good mind to make a holler to the judges. Word of this condition of affairs soon reached Mr. Marx.

"The old nut is ravin' all over the place about how he couldn't get a bet down on Elisha. Says if he wasn't allowed to bet on the best horse in his barn he certainly ain't goin' to bet on the worst one. Oh, yes, and he's talkin' about makin' a holler to the judges!"

"Fat chance!" chuckled Marx, and Jeremiah went to 25 to 1.

Clear and high above the hum of the betting ring rose the notes of a bugle. The last field of the season was being called to the track and instead of the usual staccato summons the bugler blew "Taps."

"There she goes, boys!" bellowed the bookmakers. "That's good-by for a whole year, you know! Bet 'em fast! They're on the way to the post! Only a few minutes more!"

The final attack closed in around the stands. Men who had solemnly promised themselves not to make another bet caught the fever and hurled themselves into the jam, bent on exchanging coin of the realm for pasteboard tickets and hope of sudden prosperity. It was the last race of the season, wasn't it, and good-bye to the bangtails for another year!

During this mad attack Abie squirmed through the mob and plucked at Marx's sleeve. It was his third report.

"The old bird is settin' out there in the corner of the stall all by himself, chewin' a straw. Says he's so disgusted he don't care if he sees the race or not. I started to kid him about bein' such a crab and, honest, I was afraid he'd bite me!"

Mr. Marx grinned and chalked up 40 to 1 on Jeremiah. "Now let him bleed!" said he.

The distance of the final event was three-quarters of a mile and the crowd in the betting ring continued to swarm about the stands until the clang of the gong warned them that the race was on. Then there was a wild rush for the lawn; even the fat Mr. Marx climbed down from his perch and waddled out into the sunshine, blinking as he turned his small eyes toward the back stretch.

Now little Mose had been watching the starter carefully and had thrown his mount at the barrier just as it rose in the air, but there were other jockeys in the race who had done the same thing, and Jeremiah's was not the only early speed that sizzled down to the half-mile pole. At least four of the "good things" were away to a running start—Fireball, Sky Pilot, Harry Root, and Resolution. Jeremiah trailed the quartet, content to kick clods at the second division. On the upper turn Fireball and Harry Root found the pace too warm for them and dropped back. Jeremiah found himself in third place, coasting along easily under a strong pull. The presiding judge turned his binoculars upon the black horse and favoured him with a searching scrutiny.

"Ah, hah!" said he, wagging his head. "I thought as much. Jeremiah may have bled this morning, but he ain't bleeding *now* and that little nigger is almost breaking his jaw to keep him from running over the two in front!... Old Man Curry again! Oh, but he's a cute rascal!"

"I'd rather see him get away with it than some of these other owners, at that," said the associate judge.

"So would I … I kind of like the old coot…. Now what on earth do you suppose he's done to that horse since this morning?"

A few thousand spectators were asking variations of the same question, but one spectator asked no questions at all. The Bald-faced Kid was reduced by stuttering degrees to dumb amazement. He had ignored Old Man Curry's kindly suggestion and had persuaded all and sundry to plunge heavily on Fireball.

It really was not much of a contest. Sky Pilot, on the rail, swung wide turning into the stretch and carried Resolution with him. Like a flash Little Mose shot the black horse through the opening and straightened away for the wire, an open length away for the wire, an open length in the lead.

"Come git him, jocks!" shrilled Mose. "Come git ol' Jeremiah to-day!"

The most that can be said for the other jockeys is that they tried, but Little Mose hugged the rail and Jeremiah came booming down the home stretch alone, fighting for his head and hoping for some real competition which never quite arrived. The black horse won by three open lengths, won with wraps still on his jockey's wrists, and, as the form chart stated, "did not bleed and was never fully extended."

"Well, anyhow," said Mr. Marx, as he wheezed back to his place of business, "Curry won't get anything but the purse again and that'll help some. If he brought a dead horse around here in a wagon, the best he'd get from me would be 1 to 2!"

The judges, of course, were curious. They invited Old Man Curry into the stand to ask him if he had bet on Jeremiah.

"Gentlemen," said he, removing his battered slouch hat, "I give you my word, I never went near that betting ring but once to-day, and that was to bet on a *real* hoss. 'Elisha!' I says, and I shoved it at 'em. Judges, they laughed at me. They wouldn't take a cent. Not a cent! And I was so mad——"

"Yes, yes," said the presiding judge, soothingly, "but how do you account for Jeremiah bleeding in his work this morning and running such a good race this afternoon?"

"Gentlemen," said Old Man Curry, "I don't account for it. Solomon was the smartest man that ever lived, I reckon, and there was a lot of things he never figured out. I reckon now, if he'd been in this business——"

"Good-bye, Mr. Curry," said the presiding judge, "and good luck!"

The Bald-faced Kid might see miracles with his eyes, but there was that about him which demanded explanation. Chastened in spirit, utterly humble and cast down, he called upon Old Man Curry. He found him seated in his tackle- room, reading the Old Testament by the light of a lantern.

"Come in, Frank.... Got the Lunacy Board with you?"

"Don't rub it in. And if you can spare the time, I wish you'd tell me what you've been up to with Jeremiah."

"Oh, Jeremiah. Well, now, he's a better hoss than some folks think. There wasn't anything wrong with him but just them little bleedin' spells. When I got him cured of those——"

"Cured! Was he cured this morning? Didn't I see him bleed all over the place?"

"You saw some blood, yes ... Frank, I wish't you wouldn't interrupt me when I'm talkin'.... Well, about three weeks ago I met up with a man that claimed he had a remedy to cure bleeders. I let him try his hand on Jeremiah and he done a good job. Since then we've been workin' the black rascal at two in the mornin' when all you wise folks was in bed.... Of course, I didn't want anybody to know it was Jeremiah I was figurin' on, so I gave 'em something else to think about. I started 'Lisha the same day and I tried to get as many folks interested in him as I could. I had the little nigger send him a mile so fast that a wayfarin' man and a fool couldn't help but see he was ready. And then I kind of distracted 'em some more by goin' into the bettin' ring with a big mess of one dollar bills with a fifty on the outside. I held the money up where everybody could see it and I carried on scandalous when the bookmakers wouldn't take it, I'd have carried on a lot worse if one of them children of Israel had called my bluff. And then I got so mad because they wouldn't let me bet on 'Lisha that they thought I'd lost interest in Jeremiah…. I've heard that Jeremiah wasn't played. He was played all over the ring, two dollars at a time and it was my money that played him. But of course those bookmakers knew I was sulkin' out in the paddock and took the sucker money…. Anything else you want to know?"

"Yes!" The Bald-faced Kid had reached the bursting point. "Was Jeremiah bleeding this morning or not?"

Old Man Curry stroked his beard thoughtfully.

"Well, it was real *blood*, if that's what you want to know," said he. "It took me some time to study that out. Last week Mose came around here, squawkin' on one of them little toy balloons. I took it away from him for fear it would make the hosses nervous—and then I got to studying how it was made. Last night I done some shopping. I bought a nice, fat hen and a glass pumping arrangement from a drug store…. The hen, she passed away this mornin' about daybreak. She bled quite a lot, but I got most of it in that rubber bag, and when Jeremiah was ready for his gallop——"

"You put it in his mouth?"

Old Man Curry nodded.

"Oh, why didn't you tell me?" wailed the Bald-faced Kid. "I could have cleaned up!"

"I started in to tell you, son, and you said I ought to have my head examined. And then, I kind of like to surprise folks, Frank. I knew you wouldn't have the nerve to bet on a bleeder like Jeremiah, so I had some bettin' done for you." Old Man Curry fumbled in his pocket and produced a roll of bills. "Solomon says there's a time to get, and I don't know of any better time than get-away day!"

ELIPHAZ, LATE FAIRFAX

When Old Man Curry's racing string arrived at the second stop on the Jungle Circuit the Bald-faced Kid met the horse car in the railroad yards and watched the thoroughbreds come down the chute into the corral. One by one he checked them off: Elisha, the pride of the stable; Elijah, Isaiah, Ezekiel, Esther, Nehemiah, Ruth, and Jeremiah. The aged owner, straw in mouth and hands clasped behind him, watched the unloading process narrowly giving an order now and then and sparing no more than a nod for his young friend. This sort of welcome did not discourage the Kid. He was accustomed to the old man's spells of silence, as well as his garrulous interludes.

"They look all right, old-timer," said the Kid, making conversation for its own sake. "Yes, sir, they look good. The trip didn't bother 'em much. Elisha, now, I'd say he was ready to step out and bust a track record as soon as he gets the cinders out of his ears. Shouldn't wonder if he——"

The aimless chatter died away into amazed silence. Shanghai, the hostler, appeared at the head of the chute leading a large, coal-black horse.

"Well, for Heaven's sake!" muttered the Kid, moving nearer the fence, his eyes glued on the black stranger. "Where did you pick up that fellow?... One white forefoot. H-m-m!... Say, you don't mean to tell me this is Fairfax?"

Old Man Curry nodded.

"Fairfax!" ejaculated the Bald-faced Kid disgustedly. "Well, how in the name of all that is good, great, and wise did you get that crowbait wished on you?"

Old Man Curry threw away his straw and reached for his packet of fine cut, a sure sign that he was about to unburden himself.

"He wa'n't wished on me, Frank. Jimmy Miles was stuck with a feed bill, and at the last minute, just as I was loadin' my hosses, he——"

"He stuck you with *that*," finished the Kid, pointing at the black horse.

"Well, I dunno's I'd say *stuck*," remarked Old Man Curry, looking critically at Fairfax. "Jimmy sold him to me for next to nothing."

"And you can bet he didn't misrepresent the goods any!" said the Kid. "That's exactly what Fairfax is—next to nothing. He's so near nothing that a lot of folks can't tell the difference. If you said to me: 'This is a black horse named Fairfax and that over there is nothing,' I couldn't tell which was which. Old-timer, you're in bad."

"Mebbe I am." Old Man Curry's tone was apologetic and conciliating in the extreme. "Mebbe I am. You ought to know 'bout hosses, Frank. You most gener'ly do."

"Cut out the sarcasm, because here's one I *do* know…. You made a sucker of me on Jeremiah, but don't rub it in. This Fairfax looks like a stake horse and on his breeding he ought to run like one, but he simply can't untrack himself in any kind of going. If hay was two bits a ton and this black fellow had an appetite like a humming bird, he wouldn't be worth feeding. I'm telling you!"

"I hear you, Frank." Old Man Curry pretended to reflect deeply, but there was a shifting light in his eye. "Ah, hah! Your advice, then, would be to take him out and shoot him to save expense?"

"Oh, quit your kidding, old-timer. You've bought a race horse; now go ahead and see what you can do with him."

"Well, ain't that queer?" ejaculated the old man. "Ain't it? Great minds run in the same channels, for a fact. You know, that's exackly what I was figgerin' to do! I ain't had time to look this black hoss over yet—I bought him just before we pulled out of the railroad yards—but I've been expectin' to see what I could do with him. Whenever I get hold of a hoss that ought to run—a hoss that looks as if he could run, but ain't doin' it—the next thing I want to find out is *why*. If I thought there was a cold strain in Fairfax, I wouldn't waste a minute on him, but I know he's bred right. His daddy was sure a go-getter from 'way up the creek and his mother was a nice, honest little mare and game as a badger…. And, speakin' about breeding, Frank, I don't know's you ever thought of it, but when it comes to ancestors, a real thoroughbred hoss has got something on a human being. Even Fairfax over there had his ancestors picked out for him by folks who knew their business and was after results—go back with him as far as you like and that'll be true. A hoss or a mare without class can't ring in on a family tree, whereas humans ain't noways near that partickler. Son, good looks has made grandfathers out of lots of men that by rights should have been locked up instead of married. Did you ever think of that?"

The Bald-faced Kid laughed.

"I think that you're putting up a whale of an argument to excuse yourself for shipping that black hay burner around the country. You'd save breath by admitting that Miles slipped one over on you."

"Mebbe he did and mebbe he didn't. Jimmy Miles don't know all there is to be knowed about hosses—coming right down to it, I'd say he's pretty near ignorant. Like as not he's overlooked something about this Fairfax. I tell you, on his breeding, the hoss ought to run."

"And Al Engle ought to be in jail, but he ain't. He's here, big as life."

"And aspreading himself like a green bay tree, I reckon," said the old man. "I've lopped a few branches off that rascal in my time, and if I have any luck I'll lop off a few more at this meeting.... Ole Maje Pettigrew is still the presiding judge here, ain't he?"

"Sure. They can't get rid of him."

"A lot of crooks would like to." There was a trace of grimness in the old man's tone. "Pettigrew won't stand for no monkey business, pullin' a boss's head off on Monday and cuttin' him loose on Tuesday. They've got to be middlin' consistent p'formers to get by the major, and if Al Engle goes runnin' 'em in and out he'll get his jacket dusted good; you mark what I say!"

The Bald-faced Kid shook his head.

"That's your hope talking now," said he, "and not your common sense. These race-track judges have been after The Sharpshooter a long time, but I notice he's still wearing an owner's badge and coming in at the free gate. He's a crook—no getting away from it—but he's got high-up friends."

"Let him have 'em!" snapped Old Man Curry. "You know what Solomon says? 'Though hand join in hand, the wicked shall not be unpunished.' Let Engle have his pull; it won't buy him a nickel's worth with ole Maje Pettigrew. When he starts dealin' out justice, the cards come off the top of the deck and they lay as they fall. The major will get him, I tell you!"

"I won't go into deep mourning if he does," said the Kid. "Al Engle is no friend of mine, old-timer. If he was overboard in fifty feet of water and couldn't swim a lick, I'd toss him a bar of lead—that's how much I think of him. He did me a mean trick once and I haven't got over it yet. He—say! Don't you feed that black horse, or what?"

"Huh? *Feed* him? Of course we feed him! Why?"

"You don't feed him enough or he wouldn't be trying to eat up the top rail of the fence. Take a look, will you?"

Sure enough, Fairfax was gnawing at the pine board; the grating rasp of his teeth became audible in the silence. After a time the horse dropped his head and gulped heavily.

"Suffering mackerel!" ejaculated the Kid. "He ain't really *swallowing* those splinters, is he?"

The time came when the Bald-faced Kid recalled that Old Man Curry's next remark was not a direct reply to his question. After a careful survey of the black horse the patriarch of the Jungle Circuit spoke.

"What Jimmy Miles don't know about hosses would fill a big book!"

Ten days later Fairfax, running in Old Man Curry's colours and under the name of Eliphaz, won a cheap selling race from very bad horses—won it in a canter after leading all the way. The Bald-faced Kid, a student to whom past performance was a sacred thing, was shocked at this amazing reversal of form and sought Old Man Curry—and information.

"I don't know how you do it!" said the youth. "All I can say is that you're a marvel—a wizard. This Fairfax——"

"Eliphaz, son," said the old man. "Eliphaz. I got his name changed."

"And his heart too," said the Kid. "And maybe you got him a new set of legs, or lungs, or something? Well, Eliphaz, then—do you know how fast that bird stepped the first half mile?"

Old Man Curry nodded.

"I reckon I do," said he simply. "I bet quite a chunk on him."

"But of course you wouldn't open up and tell a friend!" The Bald-faced Kid was beginning to show signs of exasperation. "You're the fellow that invented secrets, ain't you, old-timer? You're by a clam out of an oyster, you are! Never mind! Don't say it! I can tell by the look in your eye that Solomon thought the clam was the king of beasts. What I want to know is this: how did that black brute come to change his heart at the same time with his name?"

"I dunno's there was ever anything wrong with his *heart*," said Old Man Curry. "Lots of folks make that mistake and think a man's heart is bad when it's only his habits that need reformin'. Now Eliphaz, on his breeding, he ought to——"

"Yes, yes! I know all about his breeding—by Stormcloud out of Frippery—but he never ran to his breeding before. The way he ran for Jimmy Miles you'd have thought he was by a steam roller out of a wheelbarrow. What in Sam Hill have you been doing to him—sprinkling powders on his tongue?"

The old man's eyes flashed wrathfully.

"You know better'n that, Frank. All the help the black hoss had was what little bit Mose give him after the barrier went up. Ketch me handing the drug habit to a dumb critter! I guess *not*!"

"Keep your shirt on," was the soothing reply. "I'm only telling you what they say. They think Jimmy Miles didn't know the right prescription."

"A lot of things he don't know besides p'scriptions!" retorted Old Man Curry, still nettled. "Hosses, for one!"

"But you're getting away from the subject, old-timer. Ain't you going to tell me what you've done to this horse to make him win?"

"Some day, Frank—some day." The aged horseman combed his white beard with his fingers and regarded his impatient young friend with benign tolerance. "You—got many clients, so far?" Thus tactfully did Old Man Curry recognise the fact that the Bald-faced Kid was what another man might have called a tout.

"A few, yes," said the Kid. "Pikers."

"Well, sort of whisper to 'em that Eliphaz'll be a good bet the next time out."

"If it's a dog race, there won't be any price on him," was the sulky response.

"It won't be a dog race," said Old Man Curry. "It'll be a hoss race."

A few days afterward the Bald-faced Kid picked up the overnight entry slip and there found something which caused him to emit a long, low whistle.

"Well, the poor old nut!" murmured the Kid. "Just because he thinks well of the black horse, he's got no license to slip him in against the real ones…. Too much class here for Eliphaz. He may be able to beat dogs and nonwinners, but Topaz and Miss Louise will run the eyeballs out of him. Let's see—Topaz won his last start——" and the Bald-faced Kid fell to thumbing his form charts.

Topaz and Miss Louise did not run the eyeballs out of Eliphaz; the supposed contenders never got near enough to the black horse to give him a race. Eliphaz burst out in front when the barrier rose and stayed there, triumphantly kicking clods in the faces of his pursuers. To quote from the form chart notes: "Eliphaz much too good; surprised the talent by winning as he pleased."

He certainly surprised the Bald-faced Kid, and grieved him too, for that youth had persuaded a most promising client to bet his last dollar on Topaz. Topaz was second, which was some consolation, but the horse without any license to start in such company passed under the wire with three lengths to spare, his mouth wide open because of a strong pull. That night Old Man Curry poured vinegar into the wound.

"Well, son," said he, "I hope and trust you remembered what I said and cashed in on the black hoss to-day. They was offerin' 10 to 1 on him in the openin' betting. He's an improved hoss, ain't he?"

"He's *another* horse!" grunted the Kid. "Mose had to choke him all the way down the stretch to keep him from breaking a track record! What on earth have you done to him?"

"That's what they'd all like to know," chuckled the old man. "'A word spoken in due season, how good it is!' I spoke one a few days ago. Did you heed it, Frank?"

"How in hell could I figure him to beat Topaz?" snarled the Kid. "On his past performance he ain't even in the same class with horses like he beat to-day!"

Old Man Curry smiled and returned to Solomon.

"'A scorner seeketh wisdom and findeth it not, but knowledge is easy unto him that understandeth.'"

"Yes—'unto him that understandeth!' That's the point; I don't understand. Nobody understands. Here's a dead horse come to life and he's got everybody guessing. Miracles are all right, but I'm never going to bet on one until I know how it's done. Say, old-timer, ain't you going to tell me what's happened to Eliphaz?"

"No, but I'll tell you what Solomon says 'bout a loose tongue, my son." Old Man Curry paused, for he was addressing the vanishing coat tails of a much-disgusted young man. The Bald-faced Kid took himself off in a highly inflamed state of mind, and the patriarch, looking after him, shook his head sorrowfully.

"'How much better is it to get wisdom than gold,'" he quoted, "but Frank, now—he wants 'em both at the same time!"

There were others who were earnest in their search for information, which became acute when Eliphaz, late Fairfax, won his fourth race, a brilliant victory over the best horses at the track. Among the seekers after knowledge, were Al Engle and Martin O'Connor, horsemen and turf pirates with whom Old Man Curry had been at war for some time. Engle, sometimes called The Sharpshooter, was the chief conspirator; O'Connor was his lieutenant. Engle, who was responsible for the skirmishes with Curry, had begun operations with the theory that Old Man Curry was a harmless, brainless individual, "shot full of luck," he expressed it. Circumstances had caused him to alter his opinion somewhat; he no longer pitied the owner of Eliphaz and Elisha; he suspected him. O'Connor went even farther. He respected and feared everything bearing the Curry tag, the latter feeling amounting almost to superstition.

These two unworthies discussed the resurrection of Fairfax, the place of the confab being O'Connor's tackle-room and the time being the night following the fourth straight victory of the Curry colours as borne by Eliphaz.

"If it ain't hop he's using on that horse," said O'Connor, "I wish you'd tell me what it is. A month ago Fairfax was a bum; now he's pretty near a stake horse and getting better every time he starts. Why couldn't we have a smart 'vet' look him over on the sly before he goes to the post the next time? Then we could send word to the judge that Curry was stimulating the horse and———"

"And create a lovely precedent," sneered Engle. "Use your head a little more; that's what it's for. A man that hops his horses as often as you do can't afford to start any investigations along that line. If you must throw something at Curry, throw a brick, not a boomerang…. And somehow I don't believe it's hop. Fairfax was probably a good horse all the time, but Jimmy Miles didn't know it; and, as for training, Jimmy couldn't train a goat for a butting contest, let alone a thoroughbred for a race! Curry is a wise horseman—I'll give the old scoundrel that much—and he's got this bird edged up. Take it from me, he's a cracking good selling plater. I'd like to have him in my barn."

O'Connor laughed unpleasantly. He resented Engle's easy and arrogant assumption of mental superiority, and was thankful for a chance to remind The Sharpshooter of one skirmish in which all the honours had gone to Old Man Curry.

"G'wan, run him up like you did Elisha," said O'Connor. "Grab him out of a selling race. My memory ain't what it used to be, Al, but seems to me you took one of Curry's horses away from him and framed him up for a killing. Did I dream it, or did the skate run last? Go on and grab another horse away from the old boy!"

"Will you ever quit beefing about the money you lost on that race?" snapped Engle.

"Will I ever forget who got me into it?" countered O'Connor. "And if you'll take a tip from me—which you won't because you think you're smarter than I am—you'll let Old Man Curry's horses alone. It ain't in the cards that you or me can monkey with those Bible horses without getting hurt. Grab this Fairfax, or whatever they call him now, but count me out."

"No-o," said The Sharpshooter, his lips pursed and his brow wrinkled. "I don't want to grab him. I'd rather get him some other way."

"Buy him, then."

Engle shook his head.

"Curry wouldn't sell—not to me, anyway. He might to some one else. I saw Jimmy Miles this afternoon, and he was crying about what a wonderful horse he'd sold for nothing. I wonder where I could get hold of Jimmy?"

The following evening the Bald-faced Kid called upon his aged friend and interrupted a heart-to-heart session in Old Man Curry's tackle-room.

"Hello, old-timer! Hello, Jimmy! Am I butting in here?"

Jimmy Miles, a thin, sandy-haired man with pale-blue eyes and a retreating chin, answered for both.

"No, nothing private. I've been tryin' to tell Curry here that he kind of took a mean advantage of me when he bought Fairfax so cheap."

"Eliphaz," corrected the old man, "and it wa'n't no advantage because you was crazy to sell."

"I'd been drinkin' or I wouldn't have been such a fool," whined Miles. "Booze in—brains out: the old story. If I hadn't been right up against it, I wouldn't have sold the horse at all—attached to him the way I was. I'd worked with him a long time, gettin' him ready to win, and it was a mistake to let him go just when he was shapin' up. I—I'd like to buy him back. Put a price on him, old man."

Miles stooped to extinguish a burning match end which the Kid had thrown on the floor, and in that instant the Bald-faced Kid caught Old Man Curry's eye and shook his head ever so slightly.

"He ain't for sale," said the owner of Eliphaz.

"Not for cash—and your own figure?" persisted Miles. Again a wordless message flashed across the tackle-room. This time the Kid, yawning, stretched one hand high over his head.

"Two thousand dollars!" said Old Man Curry promptly.

Miles gulped his astonishment.

"Why—why, you *got* him for a hundred and fifty!" he cried.

"He's a better hoss than when I got him," said the old man, "and he's won four races. Maybe he'll win four more. You asked for my figure. You got it. Two thousand. Not a cent less."

Miles argued and pleaded, but the old man was firm.

"It ain't as if I was wantin' to sell," he explained. "I never want to sell—when the other man wants to buy. That's business, ain't it? Two thousand—take it or leave it."

"I'll see you later," said Miles. "You might come down some."

Hardly was he out of the room before Old Man Curry turned to his remaining guest.

"Well, Frank," said he, "you know something. What is it?"

"I know Miles is trying to buy the black horse for Al Engle."

Old Man Curry's fist thumped upon his knee.

"Engle! How did you find that out, son?"

The Bald-faced Kid grinned.

"Everybody ain't as close-mouthed as you are, old-timer. Engle, O'Connor, and Jimmy Miles split a quart of wine in the restaurant under the grand stand after the last race to-day and the waiter hung around and got an earful. O'Connor was against the deal from the jump. He says nobody can win any money on a Bible horse without queering his luck. Engle knows you wouldn't sell to him so he sent Miles after you and told him what to say. He'd like to run that horse in his colours next Saturday and win the Handicap with him."

"You're sure he ain't intending to lay him up with the books and have him pulled, or something?"

"Not at this track, old-timer. You see, Engle is just the least little bit leery of Pettigrew. They talked it all over and decided that it wouldn't be healthy for him to buy a four-time winner and make a bad showing with him the first time out. He wants the horse for a gambling tool, all right enough, but he won't be foolish enough to do any cheating with Eliphaz at this track. Engle says himself that he don't dare take a chance—not with old Pettigrew laying for him—on general principles. Engle thinks that if he buys the black horse and wins a good race with him first time out it may pull the wool over Pettigrew's eyes. He says Eliphaz is a cinch in the Handicap next Saturday."

Old Man Curry fingered his beard for some time in silence.

"Blast the luck!" said he suddenly. "Why didn't I know Miles was arepresentin' Al Engle?"

"You'd have said three thousand, eh?"

"No," said Old Man Curry. "No, son. Fifteen hundred."

"*Fifteen hundred!* You're crazy!"

"Mebbe I am, but Solomon, he says that even a fool, if he keeps his mouth shut tight enough, can pass for a wise man…. Frank, I wish you'd go out and find Jimmy Miles. Sort of hint to him that if he comes back here he won't be throwed out on his head. Do that for me, and mebbe you won't lose nothing by it."

The negotiations for the purchase of Eliphaz were long drawn out, but on Friday evening at dusk Old Man Curry went into the stall and said good-bye to his four-time winner.

"Don't be so skittish!" said the old gentleman. "I ain't come to put the strap on ye…. Habit is a great thing, black hoss, a great thing. In this case I'm kind of dependin' on it. You know what the dog done, don't ye? And the sow that was washed, she went wallerin' in the mire, first chance she got. That's in the New Testament, but Peter, he got the notion from Solomon and didn't give him credit either…. Good-bye, black hoss, and whatever happens, good luck!"

This was at dusk, but it was close to eleven o'clock when the transaction was completed by transfer of a fat roll of bills, which Old Man Curry counted very carefully.

"Four hundred—five hundred—Jimmy, this hoss has got a engagement for the Handicap to-morrow—seven hundred—seven-fifty—Was you thinkin' of startin' him?"

"M—well, yes. I think he's got a chance," said Miles.

"A royal chance—'Leven hundred—twelve hundred…. In that case, price bein' satisfactory and all, I oughtn't to hold out any info'mation. This black hoss shouldn't be worked to-morrow mornin'. He got his last workout to-day; the full distance, and he's ready. I wasn't even goin' to warm him up before takin' him to the paddock. Some hosses run better hot; some run better cold…. Fourteen hundred—fifteen hundred, and O. K.—Better not forget that, Jimmy."

"I won't, old-timer. Guess I better take him now, eh?"

"As well now as any other time. He's your hoss."

Major Ewell Duval Pettigrew was an early riser, but he was barely into his trousers when a bell boy tapped at his door. The major was small and plump, with a face like a harvest moon, if you can imagine a harvest moon wearing a bristling moustache and goatee. Horsemen knew to their sorrow that the major owned a long memory, a short temper, and strong prejudices. Consistent racing was his cry and woe to the in-and-outer.

"Somebody to see me, eh?" sputtered the major. "Blankety blank it to blank! Man can't even get his breakfast in peace! Oh, Mr. Curry. Show the gentleman up, boy."

"Judge," said Old Man Curry, after shaking hands, "there's something you ought to know. I bought that Eliphaz hoss from Jimmy Miles—bought him cheap."

"And a good bargain, suh," remarked Major Pettigrew.

"Mebbe. Well, Miles has been pesterin' me for a week wantin' to buy the hoss back. Said he never would have sold him if he hadn't been in licker. He kind of thought I took advantage of him, he said, but it wa'n't true, judge, not a word of it. So last night I let him buy the hoss back—for cash. This mornin' the hoss is in Al Engle's barn."

"Ah!" Major Pettigrew twisted his goatee until it stuck out straight from his chin. "Engle, eh?"

"He knew I never would have sold that hoss to him, so he sent Miles," explained Old Man Curry. "I—I've had some trouble with Engle, judge. I beat him a few times when he wasn't lookin' for me to win. In case anything happens, I thought I better see you and explain how Engle got hold of the hoss—through another party."

"Yes, suh," said Major Pettigrew. "I understand yo' position perfectly, suh. Suppose, now, you had not sold the animal. Would you say he had a chance to win the Handicap?"

"Judge," said Old Man Curry earnestly, "I would have bet on him from hell to breakfast. Now I don't know's I would put a nickel on him."

"Neither would I, suh. And, speaking of breakfast, Mr. Curry, will yo' join me in a grilled kidney?"

"Thank you just the same, judge, but I reckon I better be gettin' back to the track. I had my breakfast at sunup. I thought you ought to know the straight of how this black hoss come to change owners."

"I am indebted to you, suh," said the major, with a bow.

Jockey Merritt, wearing Engle's colours, stood in the paddock stall eyeing Eliphaz and listening to the whispered instructions of the new owner.

"Get him away flying, jock, and never look back. He's a fast breaker. Keep him in front all the way, but don't win too far."

"Bettin' much on him?" asked Merritt.

"Not a nickel. He opened at even money and they played him to 4 to 5. I don't fancy the odds, but you ride him just the same as if the last check was down— mind that. On his workout yesterday morning he's ready for a better race than any he's shown so far, so bring him home in front."

The bugle blared, the jockeys were flung into the saddles and the parade began. The race was at seven-eighths, and as the horses passed the grand stand on the way to the post Jockey Merritt heard his name called. Major Pettigrew was standing on the platform in front of the pagoda, bawling through a megaphone.

"Boy, bring that black hoss over here!"

Merritt reined Eliphaz across the track, touched the visor of his cap with his whip, and looked up inquiringly.

"Son," said Major Pettigrew, "you're on the favourite, so don't make any mistakes with him. I want to see you ride from start to finish—and I'm goin' to be watchin' you. That's all."

"I'll do my best, judge," was Merritt's answer.

"You see that the hoss does his best," warned the major. "Proceed with him, son."

The Handicap was a great race, but we are concerned with but one horse—Eliphaz, late Fairfax. When the barrier rose Jockey Merritt booted the spurs home and tried to hurl the big black into the lead. He might as well have tried to get early speed out of a porpoise. Eliphaz grunted loudly and in exactly five lumbering jumps was in last place; the other horses went on and left the favourite snorting in the dust. Jockey Merritt raked the black sides with his spurs and slashed cruelly with his whip—the favourite would not, could not get out of a slow, awkward gallop.

"Blankety blank it!" exclaimed Major Pettigrew to the associate judge. "What did I tell you, eh? Sure as a gun, Engle laid him up, and the books made him favourite and took in a ton of money! Look at him, will you? Ain't that pitiful?"

"He runs like a cow," said the major's assistant. "Merritt is certainly riding him, though. He's whipping at every jump."

It was a long way around the track, and probably only one man was really sorry for Eliphaz. Old Man Curry, at the paddock gate, shook his head as the black horse floundered down the stretch, last by fifty yards, the blunt spurs tearing at his sides and the rawhide raising welts on his shoulders.

The winning numbers had dropped into position before Eliphaz came under the wire. Major Pettigrew took one look at the horse and called to the official messenger.

"Find Engle and tell him I want to see him!"

"Well, old-timer, here we are again with our hat in our hand!" It was the Bald-faced Kid, at the door of Old Man Curry's tackle-room. "This time you've put one over for fair! Major Pettigrew has just passed out his decision to the newspaper boys."

"Ah, hah!" said the old man, looking up from the Book of Proverbs. "His decision, eh? Was he—kind of severelike?"

"Oh, no—o! Not what you'd call severe. I suppose he could have ordered

Engle boiled in oil or hung by the neck or something like that, but the major let him down light. All he did was to rule him off the turf for life!"

"Gracious Peter! You don't tell me!"

"Yes, and his horses too. The whole bunch! Engle is almost crazy. He swears on his mother's grave that he's in-no-cent and he's going to appeal to the Jockey Club and have Eliphaz examined by a 'vet' and the Lord knows what all. Oh, he's wild! It seems that Pettigrew wanted him to prove that he'd backed the horse and he couldn't produce the losing tickets. If Merritt hadn't half killed the horse, Pettigrew would have got him too."

"Well, well!" said the old man, turning back to Proverbs. "I was just readin' something here. 'He that seeketh mischief, it shall come unto him.' Engle has been seekin' mischief a long time now and look what he's got."

"Too true, old-timer," said the Bald-faced Kid, "but who was it ordered the mischief wrapped up and delivered to him? Come through!"

"Hold up your right hand!" said Old Man Curry.

"Cross my heart and hope to die if I ever tell!" said the Kid. "Now then, come clean."

"Frank," said the old man, "do you remember when we was unloadin' the hosses and ketched Eliphaz bitin' at the fence?… You do? Then you ought to be ashamed to ask any questions, because if you know hosses like you should know 'em—in your business—you wouldn't need to ask questions.

"Eliphaz is a cribber, and a cribber is a hoss that sucks itself full of wind like a balloon. I knew the minute I see him drop his head and swallow that way that cribbin' was what ailed him. That explained his bein' such a bad race hoss. Jimmy Miles probably never done a thing to correct that habit—didn't know he had it, likely.

"Well, the first thing I did was to keep the hoss's head tied high in the daytime, because no hoss will crib unless he can get his head down. Then at night I put on a cribbin' strap and buckled it tight around his neck. He could get his head down all right, but he couldn't suck any air. With that habit corrected, Eliphaz was a great hoss.

"When I found out that Engle wanted to buy him, I let Eliphaz crib all day Friday, after he'd been worked, and when I sold him I didn't sell the strap. That's all, Frank. When he went to the post he was so full of air that if Merritt hadn't been settin' on him he'd have gone up like a balloon. That's why I warned you not to let anybody bet on him…. Did you do pretty well, Frank?"

"I got a toothful while some other folks was getting a meal," answered the

Kid. "Just one thing more: where did you get that name—Eliphaz?"

"That was a sort of a joke," confessed the old man. "Once there was a party named Job, and he had all sorts of hard luck. Some of that hard luck was in not bein' able to lose his friends. They used to come and see him and hold a lodge of sorrow and set on the ground and talk and talk—whole chapters of talk—and the windiest one of 'em all——"

"I get you!" chuckled the Bald-faced Kid. "That was Eliphaz!"

Old Man Curry nodded.

"'Knowledge is easy unto him that understandeth,'" he quoted.

"Yes, but an inside tip now and then never hurt anybody," said the Bald-faced Kid. "Declare me in on the next miracle, will you?"

THE REDEMPTION HANDICAP

"Well, old sport, are you going to slip another one over on 'em to-day?"

"What do you think of Jeremiah's chances, Mr. Curry?"

"Can this black thing of yours beat the favourite?"

"There's even money on Jeremiah for a place; shall I grab it?"

Old Man Curry, standing at the entrance to a paddock stall, lent an unwilling ear to these queries. He was a firm believer in the truth, but more firmly he believed in the fitness of time and place. The whole truth, spoken incautiously in the paddock, has been known to affect closing odds, and it was the old man's habit to wager at post time, if at all. Those who pestered the owner of the "Bible stable" with questions about the fitness of Jeremiah and his chances to be first past the post went back to the betting ring with their enthusiasm for the black horse slightly abated. Old Man Curry admitted, under persistent prodding, that if Jeremiah got off well, and nothing happened to him, and it was one of his good days, and he didn't get bumped on the turn, and the boy rode him just right, and he could stay in front of the favourite, he might win. Pressed further, a note of pessimism developed in the patriarch's conversation; he became the bearded embodiment of reasonable doubt. Curry's remarks, rapidly circulating in the betting ring, may have made it possible for Curry's betting commissioner, also rapidly circulating at the last minute, to unload a considerable bundle of Curry's money on Jeremiah at odds of 5 and 6 to 1.

One paddock habitué, usually a keen seeker after information, might have received a hint worth money had he come after it. Old Man Curry noted the absence of the Bald-faced Kid, and when the bugle sounded the call to the track he turned the bridle over to Shanghai, the negro hostler, and ambled into the betting ring in search of his young friend. The betting ring was the Kid's place of business—if touting is classed as an occupation and not a misdemeanour—but Old Man Curry did not find him in the crowd. It was not until the horseman stepped out on the lawn that he spied the Kid, his elbows on the top rail of the fence, his chin in his hands, and his back squarely turned to the betting ring. He did not even look around when the old man addressed him.

"Well, Frank, I kind of expected you in the paddock."

The Kid was staring out across the track with the fixed gaze of one who sees nothing in particular; he grunted slightly, but did not speak.

"Jeremiah—he's worth a bet to-day."

"Uh-huh!" This without interest or enthusiasm.

"I saw some 5 to 1 on him just now."

The Kid swung about and glanced listlessly toward the betting ring. Then he looked at the horses on their way to the post. The old man read his thought.

"You've got a couple of minutes yet," said he. "Mebbe more; there's some bad actors in that bunch, and they'll delay the start."

The Kid looked again at the betting ring; then he shook his head. "Aw, what's the use?" said he irritably. "What's the use?"

Old Man Curry's countenance took on a look of deep concern.

"What ails you, son? Ain't you well?"

"Well enough, I guess. Why?"

"Because I never see you pass up a mortal cinch before."

The Kid chuckled mirthlessly. "Old-timer," said he, "I'm up against a cinch of my own—but it's a cinch to lose."

He returned to his survey of the open field, but Old Man Curry lingered. He stroked his beard meditatively.

"Son," said he at length, "Solomon says that a brother is born for adversity. I don't know what a father is born for, but I reckon it's to give advice. Where you been the last week or ten days? It's mighty lonesome round the stable without you."

"I'm in a jam, and you can't help me."

"Mebbe not, but it might do some good to talk it all out of your system. You know the number, Frank."

"You mean well, old-timer," said the Kid; "and your heart's in the right place, but you—you don't understand."

"No, and how can I 'less you open up and tell me what's the matter? If you've done anything wrong——"

"Forget it!" said the Kid shortly. "You're barking up the wrong tree. I'm trying to figure out how to do right!"…

That night the door of Old Man Curry's tack room swung gently open, and the aged horseman, looking up from his well-thumbed copy of the Old Testament, nodded to an expected visitor.

"Set down, Frank, and take a load off your feet," said he hospitably. "I sort of thought you'd come."

For a time they talked horse, usually an engrossing subject, but after a bit the conversation flagged. The Kid rolled many cigarettes which he tossed away unfinished, and the old man waited in silence for that which he knew could not long be delayed. It came at last in the form of a startling question. "Old- timer," said the Kid abruptly, "you—you never got married, did you?"

Old Man Curry blinked a few times, passed his fingers through his beard, and stared at his questioner. "Why, no, son." The old man spoke slowly, and it was plain that he was puzzled. "Why, no; I never did."

"Did you ever think of it—seriously, I mean?"

Old Man Curry met this added impertinence without resentment, for the light was beginning to dawn on him. He drew out his packet of fine cut and studied its wrappings carefully.

"I'm not kidding, old-timer. Did you ever think of it?"

"Once," was the reply. "Once, son, and I've been thinking about it ever since. She was the right one for me, but she got the notion I wasn't the right one for her. Sometimes it happens that way. She found the man she thought she wanted, and I took to runnin' round the country with race horses. After that she was sure I was a lost soul and hell-bent for certain. This was a long time ago—before you was born, I reckon."

After a silence, the Kid asked another question:

"Well, at that, the race-track game is no game for a married man, is it?"

"M-m-well," answered the patriarch thoughtfully, "that's as how a man's wife looks at it. Some of 'em think it ain't no harm to gamble s'long's you can win, but the average woman, Frank, she don't want the hosses runnin' for her bread and butter. You can't blame her for that, because a woman is dependent by nature. If the Lord had figured her to git out an' hustle with the men, He'd have built her different, but He made her to be p'tected and shelteredlike. A single man can hustle and bat round an' go hungry if he wants to, but he ain't got no right to ask a woman to gamble her vittles on any proposition whatever."

"Ain't it the truth!" ejaculated the Bald-faced Kid, with a depth of feeling quite foreign to his nature. "You surely spoke a mouthful then!" Old Man Curry raised one eyebrow slightly and continued his discourse.

"For a man even to figger on gettin' married, he ought to have something comin' in steady—something that bad hosses an' worse men can't take away from him. He oughtn't to bet at all, but if he does it ought to be on a mortal cinch. There ain't many real cinches on a race track, Frank; not the kind that a married man'd be justified in bettin' the rent money on. Yes, sir, a man thinkin' 'bout gettin' married ought to have a job—and stick to it!"

"And that job oughtn't to be on a race track either," supplemented the Kid, his eyes fixed on the cigarette which he was rolling. "But that ain't all I wanted to ask you about, old-timer. Suppose, now, a fellow had a girl that was too good for him—a girl that wouldn't wipe her feet on a gambler if she knew it, and was brought up to think that betting was wrong. And suppose now that this fellow wasn't even a gambler. Suppose he was a hustler—a tout—but he'd asked the girl to marry him without telling her what he was, and she'd said she would. What ought that fellow to do?"

Old Man Curry took his time about answering; took also a large portion of fine cut and stowed it away in his cheek.

"Well, son," said he gently, "it would depend a lot on which the fellow cared the most for—the race track or the girl."

The Kid flung the cigarette from him and looked up, meeting the old man's eyes for the first time. "I beat you to it, old-timer! Win or lose, I'm through at the end of this meeting. There's a fellow over in Butte just about my age. He was a hustler too, and a pal of mine, but two years ago he quit, and now he's got a little gents' furnishing-goods place—nothing swell, of course, but the business is growing all the time. He's been after me to come in with him on a percentage of the profits, and last night I wrote him to look for me when they get done running here. That part of it is settled. No more race track in mine. But that ain't what I was getting at. Have I got to tell the girl what I've been doing the last five years?"

"Would you rather have her find out from some one else, Frank?"

"No-o."

"If you want to start clean, son, the best place to begin is with the girl."

"But what if she throws me down?"

"That's the chance you'll have to take. You've been taking 'em all your life."

"Yes, but nothing ever meant as much to me as this does."

"Well, son, the more a woman cares for a man the more she'll forgive."

"Did Solomon say that?" demanded the Kid suspiciously.

"No, *I* said it. You see, Frank, it was this way with Solomon: he had a thousand wives, more or less, and I reckon he never had time to strike a general average. He wrote a lot 'bout women, first and last, but it seems he only remembered two kinds—the ones that was too good to live and the ones that wasn't worth killin'. It would have been more helpful to common folks if he'd said something 'bout the general run of women. You'd better tell her, Frank."

The Bald-faced Kid sighed.

"I'd rather take a licking. You're sure about that forgiving business, old-timer?"

"It's the one best bet, my son."

"Pull for it to go through, then. Good night—and thank you."

Left alone, Old Man Curry turned the pages for a time, then read aloud:

"'There be three things which are too wonderful for me, yea, four which I know not: The way of an eagle in the air; the way of a serpent upon a rock; the way of a ship in the midst of the sea, and the way of a man with a maid
—*the way of a man with a maid.*' Well, after all, the straight way is the best way, and the boy's on the right track."

A few days later Old Man Curry, sunning himself in the paddock, caught sight of the Kid. That engaging youth had a victim pinned in a corner and, programme in hand, was pointing the way to prosperity.

"Now, listen," he was saying; "you ain't taking a chance when you bet on this bird to-day. Didn't I tell you that the boy that rides him is my cousin? And ain't the owner my pal? What better do you want than that? This tip comes straight from the barn, and you can get 20 to 1 for all your money!"

The victim squirmed and wriggled and twisted and would have broken away but for the Kid's compelling eye. At last he thought of something to say:

"If this here Bismallah is such a hell-clinkin' good race horse, how come they ain't *all* bettin' on him?"

"Why ain't they?" the Kid fairly squealed. "Because we've been lucky enough to keep him under cover from everybody! That's why! Nobody knows what he can do; the stable money won't even be bet here for fear of tipping him off; it'll be bet in the pool rooms all over the Coast. He'll walk in, I tell you—just *walk* in! Why, say! You don't think I'd tell you this if I didn't know it was *so*? Here comes the owner. I'll go talk with him. You wait right here!"

It was really the owner of Bismallah, who, speaking out of the corner of his mouth, told the Bald-faced Kid to go to a warmer clime. The hustler returned to his victim instead.

"He says it's all fixed up; everything framed; play him across the board. Come on!"

The victim allowed himself to be dragged in the direction of the betting ring, and Old Man Curry watched the proceedings with a whimsical light in his eye. Later he found a chance to discuss the matter with the Kid. The last race was over, and Frank was through for the day.

"You're persuadin' 'em pretty *strong*, ain't you, son?" asked the old man. "You used to give advice; now you're makin' 'em *take* it whether they want to or not."

"Where do you get that stuff?" demanded the Kid, bristling immediately.

"Why, I saw you working on that big fellow in the grey suit. I was afraid you'd have to hit him on the head and go into his pocket after it. Looked to me like he wasn't exackly crazy to gamble."

"Oh, him!" The tout spat contemptuously. "Do you know what that piker wanted to bet? Six dollars, across the board! I made him loosen up for fifteen, and he howled like a wolf."

"The hoss—lost?" By the delicate inflection and the pause before the final word, Old Man Curry might have been inquiring about the last moments of a departed friend. The Kid was looking at the ground, so he missed the twinkle in the old man's eyes.

"He ran like an apple woman," was the sullen response. "Confound it, old-timer, I can't pick 'em every time!"

"No, I reckon not," said the patriarch. "I—reckon—not." He lapsed into silence.

"Aw, spit it out!" said the Kid after a time. "I'd rather hear you say it than feel you thinking it!"

Old Man Curry smiled one of his rare smiles, and his big, wrinkled hand fell lightly on the boy's shoulder.

"What I was thinking wasn't much, son," said he. "It was this: if you can make total strangers open up and spend their substance for something they only think is there, you ought to get rid of an awful lot of shirts and socks and flummery— the things that folks can see. If you can sell stuff that *ain't*, you surely can sell stuff that *is*!"

"I'm sick of the whole business!" The words ripped out with a snarl. "I used to like this game for the excitement in it—for the kick. I used to like to see 'em run. Now I don't give a damn, so long as I can get some coin together quick. And the more you need it the harder it is to get! To-day I had four suckers down on different horses in the same race, and a sleeper woke up on me. Four bets down and not a bean!"

The twinkle had gone from the old man's eyes.

"Four hosses in one race, eh? Do you need the money that bad, son?"

For answer the Kid plunged his hand into his pocket and brought out a five-dollar gold piece and a small collection of silver coins which he spread upon his palm.

"There's the bank roll," said he, "and don't tell me that Solomon pulled that line about a fool and his money!"

The old man calmly appraised the exhibit of precious metals before he spoke.

"How come you to be down so low, son?"

"I was trying to win myself out a little stake," was the sulky answer; "but they cleaned me. That's why I'm hustling so hard. It's a rotten game, but it owes me something, and I want to collect it before I quit!"

"Ah, hah!" said Old Man Curry, stroking his beard meditatively. "Ah, hah! You haven't told her yet."

"No, but I'm going to. That's honest."

"I believe you, son, but did it ever strike you that mebbe she wouldn't want you to make a fresh start on money that you got this way? Mebbe she wouldn't want to start with you."

"Dough is dough." The Bald-faced Kid stated this point in the manner of one forestalling all argument. "At one time and another I've handled quite a lot of it that I got different ways, but I never yet had any trouble passing it off on folks, and they didn't hold their noses when they took it either. Anything that'll spend is good money, and don't you forget it!"

"But this girl, now—mebbe she won't think so."

"What she don't know won't hurt her."

"Son, what a woman don't know she guesses and feels, and she may have the same sort of a feelin' that I've got—that some kinds of money never bring anybody luck. A while ago you said this game was rotten, and yet you're tryin' to cash in your stack and pick up all the sleepers before you quit. Seems to me I'd want to start *clean*."

"Dough is dough, I tell you!" repeated the Kid stubbornly. He turned and shook his fist at the distant betting ring where the cashiers were paying off the last of the winning tickets. "Look out for me, all of you sharks!" said the boy.

"From now till the end of the meeting it's packing-house rules, and everything goes!"

"'A wise son heareth his father's instruction,'" quoted Old Man Curry.

"I hear you, old-timer," said the Kid, "but I don't get you. Next thing I suppose you'll pull Solomon on me and tell me what he says about tainted money!"

"I can do that too. Let's see, how does it go? Oh, yes. 'There is that maketh himself rich, *yet hath nothing*; there is that maketh himself poor, yet hath great riches.' That's Solomon on the money question, my boy."

"Huh!" scoffed the unregenerate one. "Solomon was a king, wasn't he, with dough to burn? It's mighty easy to talk—when you've got yours. I haven't got mine yet, but you watch my smoke while I go after it!"

Old Man Curry trudged across the infield in the wake of the good horse Elisha. Another owner, on the day of an important race, might have been nervous or worried; the patriarch maintained his customary calm; his head was bent at a reflective angle, and he nibbled at a straw. Certain gentlemen, speculatively inclined, would have given much more than a penny for the old man's thoughts; having bought them at any price, they would have felt themselves defrauded.

Elisha, the star performer of the Curry stable, had been combed and groomed and polished within an inch of his life, and there were blue ribbons in his mane, a sure sign of the confidence of Shanghai, the hostler. He was also putting this confidence into words and telling the horse what was expected of him.

"See all them folks, 'Lisha? They come out yere to see you win anotheh stake an' trim that white hoss from Seattle. Grey Ghost, thass whut they calls him. When you hooks up with him down in front of that gran' stan', he'll think he's a ghost whut's mislaid his graveyard, yes, indeedy! They tells me he got lots of that ol' early speed; they tells me he kin go down to the half-mile pole in nothin', flat. Let him *do* it; 'tain't early speed whut wins a mile race; it's *late* speed. Ain't no money hung up on that ol' half-mile pole! Let that white fool run his head off; he'll come back to you. Lawdy, all them front runners comes back to the reg'lar hosses. Run the same like you allus do, an' eat 'em up in the stretch, 'Lisha! Grey Ghost—pooh! I neveh seen *his* name on no lamp-post! I bet befo' you git th'ough with him he'll wish he'd saved some that ol' early speed to finish on. You ask me, 'Lisha, I'd say we's spendin' this yere first money right *now*!"

It was the closing day of the meeting, always in itself an excuse for a crowd, but the management had generously provided an added attraction in the shape of a stake event. Now a Jungle Circuit stake race does not mean great wealth as a general thing, but this was one of the few rich plums provided for the horsemen. First money would mean not less than $2,000, which accounted for the presence of the Grey Ghost. The horse had been shipped from Seattle, where he had been running with and winning from a higher grade of thoroughbreds than the Jungle Circuit boasted, and there were many who professed to believe that the Ghost's victory would be a hollow one. There were others who pinned their faith on the slow-beginning Elisha, for he was, as his owner often remarked, "an honest hoss that always did his level best." Eight other horses were entered, but the general opinion seemed to be that there were only two contenders. The others, they said, would run for Sweeney —and third money.

Old Man Curry elbowed his way through the paddock crowd, calmly nibbling at his straw. He was besieged by men anxious for his opinion as to the outcome of the race; they plucked at the skirts of his rusty black coat; they caught him by the arms. Serene and untroubled, he had but one answer for all.

"Yes, he's ready, and we're tryin'."

In the betting ring Grey Ghost opened at even money with Elisha at 7 to 5. The Jungle speculators went to the Curry horse with a rush that almost swept the block men off their stands, and inside of three minutes Elisha was at even money with every prospect of going to odds-on, and the grey visitor was ascending in price. The sturdy big stretch-runner from the Curry barn had not been defeated at the meeting; he was the known quantity and could be depended upon to run his usual honest race.

The Ghost's owner also attracted considerable attention in the paddock. He was a large man, rather pompous in appearance, hairless save for a fringe above this ears, and answered to the name of "Con" Parker, the Con standing for concrete. He had been in the cement business before taking to the turf, and there were those who hinted that he still carried a massive sample of the old line above his shoulders. When cross-examined about the grey horse, he blunted every sharp inquiry with polite evasions, but he looked wiser than any human could possibly be, and the impression prevailed that he knew more than he would tell. Perhaps this was true.

The saddling bell rang, and the jockeys trooped into the paddock, followed by the roustabouts with the tackle. Old Man Curry, waiting quietly in the far corner of Elisha's stall, saw the Bald-faced Kid wriggling his way through the crowd. He came straight to the old man.

"Elisha's 4 to 5 now," he announced breathlessly, "and they're still playing him hard. The other one is 5 to 2. Looks like a false price on the Ghost, and I know that Parker is going to set in a chunk on him at post time. What do you think about it?"

"You goin' to bet your own money, son?"

"I've got to do it—make or break right here."

"How strong are you?"

"Just about two hundred bones."

"Ah, hah!" Old Man Curry paused a moment for thought and sucked at his straw. "Two hundred at 5 to 2—that'd make seven hundred, wouldn't it? Pretty nice little pile."

The Kid's eyes widened. "Then you don't think Elisha can beat the Ghost to-day?"

"I ain't bettin' a cent on him," said the old man. "Not a cent." And the manner in which he said it meant more than the words.

"Then, shall I—?"

Old Man Curry glanced over at the grey horse, standing quietly in his stall.

"Play that one, son," he whispered.

After the Kid had gone rocketing back to the betting ring, Curry turned to Jockey Moseby Jones.

"Mose," said he, "don't lay too far out of it to-day. This grey hoss lasts pretty well, so begin workin' on 'Lisha sooner than usual. He's ready to stand a long, hard drive. Bring him home in front, boy!"

"Sutny will!" chuckled the little negro. "At's bes' thing I do!"

When the barrier rose, a grey streak shot to the front and went skimming along the rail, opening an amazingly wide gap on the field. It was the Ghost's habit to make every post a winning one; he liked to run in front of the pack.

As he piloted the big bay horse around the first turn into the back stretch, Jockey Mose estimated the distance between his mount and the flying Ghost, taking no note of the other entries. Then he began to urge Elisha slightly.

"Can't loaf much to-day, hawss!" he coaxed. "Shake yo'self! Li'l mo' steam!"

The men who had played the Curry horse to odds on and thought they knew his running habits were surprised to see him steadily moving up on the back stretch. It was customary for Elisha to begin to run at the half-mile pole— usually from a tail-end position—but to-day he was mowing down the outsiders even before he reached that point, and on the upper turn he went thundering into second place—with the Ghost only five lengths away. The imported jockey on Parker's horse cast one glance behind him, and at the head of the stretch he sat down hard in his saddle and began hand riding with all his might. Close in the rear rose a shrill whoop of triumph.

"No white hawss eveh was *game*, 'Lisha! Sic him, you big red rascal, sic him! Make him dawg it!"

But the Ghost was game to the last ounce. More than that, he had something left for the final quarter, though his rider had not expected to draw upon that reserve so soon. The Ghost spurted, for a time maintaining his advantage. Then, annihilating incredible distances with his long, awkward strides and gathering increased momentum with every one, Elisha drew alongside. Again the Ghost was called on and responded, but the best he had left and all he had left, was barely sufficient to enable him to hold his own. Opposite the paddock inclosure, with the grand stand looming ahead, the horses were running nose and nose; ten yards more and the imported jockey drew his whip. Moseby Jones cackled aloud.

"You ain't *stuck* on 'is yere white sellin' plater, is you, 'Lisha? Whut you hangin' round him faw, then? Bid him good night *an' good-bye*!"

He drove the blunt spurs into Elisha's sides, and the big bay horse leaped out and away in a whirlwind finish that left the staggering Ghost five lengths behind and incidentally lowered the track record for one mile.

It was a very popular victory, as was attested by the leaping, howling dervishes in the grand stand and on the lawn, but there were some who took no part in the demonstration. Some, like Con Parker, were hit hard.

There was one who was hit hardest of all, a youth of pleasing appearance who drew several pasteboards from his pocket and scowled at them for a moment before he ripped them to bits and hurled the fragments into the air.

"Cleaned out! Busted!" ejaculated the Bald-faced Kid bitterly. "The old scoundrel double-crossed me!"

The last race of the meeting was over when Old Man Curry emerged from the track office of the Rating Association. The grand stand was empty, and the exits were jammed with a hurrying crowd. The betting ring still held its quota, and the cashiers were paying off the lines with all possible speed. As they slapped the winning tickets upon the spindles, they exchanged pleasantries with the fortunate holders.

"Just keep this till we come back again next season," said they. "We're lending it to you—that's all."

Old Man Curry made one brisk circle of the ring, examining every line of ticket holders, then he walked out on the lawn. The Bald-faced Kid was sitting on the steps of the grand stand smoking a cigarette. Curry went over to him. "Well, Frank," said he cheerfully, "how did you come out on the day?"

The boy stared up at him for a moment before he spoke.

"You ought to know," said he slowly. "You told me to bet on that grey horse —and then you went out and beat him to death!"

"Ah, hah!" said the old man.

"I was crazy for a minute," said the Kid. "I thought you'd double-crossed me. I've cooled out since then; now I'm only sorry that you didn't know more about what your own horse could do. That tip made a tramp out of me, old- timer."

"Exackly what I hoped it would do, son," and Old Man Curry fairly beamed.

"*What's that?*" The cigarette fell from the Kid's fingers, and his lower jaw sagged. "You thought Elisha could *win*—and you went and touted me on to the other one?"

Old Man Curry nodded, smiling.

As the boy watched him, his expression changed to one of deep disgust. He dipped into his vest pocket and produced his silver stop watch. "Here's something you overlooked," he sneered. "Take it, and I'll be cleaned right!"

Old Man Curry sat down beside him, but the Kid edged away. "I wouldn't have thought it of you, old-timer," said he.

"Frank," said the old man gently, "you don't understand. You don't know what I was figgerin' on."

"I know this," retorted the Kid: "if it hadn't been for you, I wouldn't have to go to Butte alone!"

"You've told her, then?"

"Last night."

"And I was right about the forgivin' business, son?"

"Didn't I say she was going to Butte with me? We had it all fixed to get married, but now——"

"Well, I don't see no reason for callin' it off." Old Man Curry's cheerfulness had returned, and as he spoke he drew out his old-fashioned leather wallet. "You know what I told you 'bout bad money, son—tainted money? You wouldn't take my word for it that gamblers' money brings bad luck; I just nachelly had to fix up some scheme on you so that you wouldn't have no bad money to start out with." He opened the wallet and extracted a check upon which the ink was scarcely dry—the check of the Racing Association for the winner's portion of the stake just decided. "I wouldn't want you to have bad luck, son," the old man continued. "I wanted you to have good luck—and a clean start. Here's some money that it wouldn't hurt anybody to handle—an honest hoss went out and run for it and earned it, an' he was runnin' for you every step of the way! Here, take it." He thrust the check into the boy's hand —and let it stand to his credit that he answered before looking at it.

"I—I had you wrong, old-timer," he stammered: "wrong from the start. I—I can't take this. I ain't a pauper, and I—I——"

"Why of course you can take it, son," urged the old man. "You said this game owed you a stake, and maybe it does, but the only money you can afford to start out with is clean money, and the only clean money on a race track is the money that an honest hoss can go out and run for—and win. No, I can't take it back; it's indorsed over to you."

Then, and not before, did the Kid look at the figures on the check.

"Why," he gasped, "this—this is for twenty-four hundred and something! I don't *need* that much! I—we—*she* says three hundred would be plenty! I ——"

"That's all right," interrupted Old Man Curry. "Money—clean money—never comes amiss. You can call the three hundred the stake that was owin' to you; the rest, well, I reckon that's just my weddin' present. Good-bye, son, and good luck!"

A MORNING WORKOUT

"Well, boss, they sutny done it to us again to-day. Look like it gittin' to be a *habit* on thisyere track!"

Thus, querulously, Jockey Moseby Jones, otherwise Little Mose, as he trudged dejectedly across the infield beside his employer, Old Man Curry, owner of Elisha, Elijah, Ezekiel, Isaiah, and other horses bearing the names of major and minor prophets. Mose was still in his silks—there were reasons, principally Irish, why the little negro found it more comfortable to dress in the Curry tack room—and the patriarch of the Jungle Circuit wore the inevitable rusty frock coat and battered slouch hat. Side by side they made a queer picture: the small, bullet-headed negro in gay stable colours, and the tall, bearded scarecrow, the frayed skirts of his coat flapping at his knees as he walked. Ahead of them was Shanghai, the hostler, leading a steaming thoroughbred which had managed to finish outside the money in a race that his owner had expected him to win: expected it to the extent of several hundred dollars. "Yes, suh, it gittin' to be a habit!" complained Little Mose. "Been so long since I rode into 'at ring I fo'get what it feels like to win a race!"

"It's a habit we're goin' to break one of these days, Mose. What happened!"

"Huh! Ast me whut didn't happen! Ol' 'Lijah, he got off good, an' first dash —*wham*! he gits bumped by 'at ches'nut hawss o' Dyer's. I taken him back some an' talk to him, an' jus' when I'm sendin' him again—*pow*! Jock Merritt busts ol' 'Lijah 'cross 'e nose 'ith his whip. In 'e stretch I tries to come th'oo on inside, an' two of 'em Irish jocks pulls oveh to 'e rail and puts us in a pocket. 'Niggeh,' they say to me, 'take 'at oat hound home 'e long way; you sutny neveh git him th'oo!' They was right, boss! 'Lijah, he come fourth, sewed up like a eagle in a cage!"

"H'm-m. And the judges didn't pay any attention when you claimed a foul?"

Little Mose gurgled wrathfully. "Huh! I done claim *three* fouls! Judges, they say they didn't see no foul a-a-a-tall! Didn't see us git bumped; didn't see Jock Merritt hit 'Lijah; didn't see us pocketed. 'Course they didn't; they wasn't *lookin'* faw no foul! On 'is track we not on'y got to beat hawsses; we got to beat jocks an' judges too. How we goin' lay up any bacon agin such odds as that?"

"It can't last, Mose," was the calm reply. "'There shall be no reward to the evil man; the candle of the wicked shall be put out.'"

"It burnin' mighty bright jus' now, boss. Sol'mun, he say that?"

Old Man Curry nodded, and Little Mose sniffed sceptically. "Uh huh. Sol'mun he neveh got jipped out of seven races in a row!"

"Seven, eh!" The old man counted on his fingers. "Why, so it is, Mose! This is the seventh time they've licked us, for a fact!" Old Man Curry began to chuckle, and the jockey eyed him curiously.

"You sutny enjoy it mo'n I do, boss," said he.

"That's because you don't read Solomon," replied the owner. "Listen: 'A just man falleth seven times and riseth up again.' Mose, we're due to rise up and smite these Philistines."

"Huh! Why not smite some 'em Irish boys first? You reckon 'em crooked judges kin see us when we risin' up?"

"We'll have to fix it so's they can't overlook us, Mose."

"Ought to git 'em some eyeglasses then," was the sulky response.

"Seven and one—that's eight, Mose. We've got Solomon's word for it."

Jockey Moseby Jones shook his head doubtfully. "Mebbe so, boss, mebbe so, but thisyere Sol'mun's been dead a lo-o-ng time now. He neveh got up agin a syndicate bettin' ring an' crooked judgin'. He neveh rode no close finish 'ith Irish jocks an' had his shin barked on 'e fence. You kin take Sol'mun's word faw it, boss, but li'l Moseby, he's f'um Mizzoury. He'll steal a flyin' start nex' time out an' try to stay so far in front that no Irish boy kin reach him 'ith a lariat!"

A big, jovial-looking man, striding rapidly toward the stables, overtook them from the rear and announced his presence by slapping Old Man Curry resoundingly on the back. "Tough luck!" said he with a grin. "Awful tough luck, but you can't win all the time, you know, old-timer!"

"Why, yes," said Curry quietly; "that's a fact, Johnson. Nobody but a hog would want to win *all* the time. And I wish you wouldn't wallop me on the back thataway. I most nigh swallered my tobacco."

Johnson laughed loudly. "How do you like our track?" he asked.

"Your track is all right," answered the old man, with just a shade of emphasis placed where it would do the most good. "A visitor don't seem to do very well here, though," he added.

"The fortunes of war!" chuckled Johnson.

"Ah, hah," said Curry. "My boy here can tell you 'bout that. He says the other jockeys fight him all the way round the track."

"Well," said Johnson, "you know why that is, don't you? The boys ain't stuck on his colour, and you can't blame 'em for that, Curry. If you had a boy like Walsh, now, it would be different."

"I'll bet it would!" was the emphatic response of Old Man Curry.

"I think I can get Walsh for you."

"No-o." Old Man Curry dropped his hand on the negro's shoulder. "No. Mose has been ridin' for me quite some time now. He suits me first rate."

"You're the doctor," grinned Johnson. "Do as you think best, of course. I'm only telling you how it is."

"Thankee. I reckon I'll play the string out the way I started. Luck might change."

"Yes, it'll run bad for a while and then turn right round and get worse. So long!" Johnson hurried on toward the stables, laughing loudly at his ancient jest, and Old Man Curry looked after him with a meditative squint in his eyes.

"'As the crackling of thorns under a pot,'" he quoted soberly. "A man that laughs all the time ain't likely to mean it, Mose, but I don't know's I would say that Johnson is exackly a fool. No, he's a pretty wise man, of his breed. He owns a controllin' interest in this track (under cover, of course), he's got a couple of books in the ring, and the judges are with him. I reckon from what he said 'bout Walsh that he's in with the jockey syndicate. No wonder he wins races! Sure, he could get Walsh for me, or any other crook-legged little burglar that would send word to Johnson what I was doing! Mose, yonder goes the man we've got to beat!"

"Him too, boss?" Little Mose rolled his eyes. "Hawsses, judges, jocks, an' Johnson! Sutny is a tough card to beat!"

"'A just man falleth seven times and riseth up again,'" repeated the old man, "'but the wicked shall fall into mischief.' That's the rest of the verse, Mose."

"Boss," said the little negro earnestly, "I don' wish nobody no hard luck, but if somebody got to fall, I hope one of them Irish jocks will fall in front an' git jumped on by ten hawsses!"

"Don't make any mistake about it, Curry is wise. He may look like a Methodist preacher gone to seed, but the old scoundrel knows what's going on. He ain't a fool, take it from me!"

The speaker was Smiley Johnson, who was addressing a small but extremely select gathering of turf highwaymen who had met in his tackle-room to discuss matters of importance. They were all men who would willingly accept two tens for a five or betray a friend for gain: Smiley Johnson, Billy Porter, Curly McManus, and Slats Wilson. All owned horses and ran them in and out of the money, as they pleased, and not one of them would have trusted the others as far as a bull may be thrown by the tail.

"We can trim the old reprobate," continued Johnson, "but we can't keep him from finding out that the clippers are on him."

"And who cares if he does know?" demanded Slats Wilson. "I'm in favour of making it so raw that he'll take his horses and go somewhere else. Look at what he did last season. Got Al Engle and a lot of other people ruled off, didn't he? Raised particular hell all over the circuit, the psalm-singing old hypocrite!"

"He's got a fine, fat chance to get anybody ruled off around this track," interrupted Curly McManus. "These judges ain't reformers. They know who's paying their salaries."

"Sure they do," assented Wilson, "but the longer this old rip hangs on the more chance there is to get into a jam of some kind. He's a natural-born trouble maker. If he loses many more races the way he lost that one to-day, I wouldn't put it past him to go to the newspapers with a holler. That would hurt. I'm in favour of giving him the gate!"

"When he hasn't won a race?" argued Johnson. "Use your head, Slats. Let him run his horses, and bet on 'em. He may squawk, but he can't prove anything, and when he's lost enough dough he'll quit."

"Is there any way that we could frame up and get him ruled off?" asked Porter.

"The ruling wouldn't stand," said Johnson. "Curry has got too many friends higher up, and if we should try it and fall down it would give the track a black eye. The sucker horsemen would be leery of us."

"If any framing is to be done," announced McManus, "count me out now. You fellows know Grouchy O'Connor? Him and Engle framed on Curry till they were black in the face, and what did it get 'em? Not a nickel's worth! You've got to admit that Al Engle was smart as they make 'em, but O'Connor tells me that Curry made Al look like a selling-plater: had him outguessed at every turn on the track. Let Curry run his horses, and our boys will take care of the little nigger."

"That Elisha is quite a horse," commented Johnson. "If they take care of him, they'll go some."

"What's the use of worrying about Elisha?" asked McManus. "Curry hasn't started him yet at the meeting. He's trying to pick up some dough with Elijah and Isaiah and the others. They ain't so very much."

"Well, Elijah would have been right up there to-day if it hadn't been for a little timely interference now and then." Johnson grinned broadly as he spoke.

"A little timely interference!" ejaculated Wilson. "The boys did everything to that horse but knock him over the fence!"

"And the judges didn't see a thing!" chuckled Johnson.

"Say, let's get down to business!" said Porter. "What I want to know is this, Johnson: when are you going to cut loose with Zanzibar? You said we'd all be in with that; there'll be a sweet price on him, and we ought to clean up."

"Zanzibar is about ready," answered Johnson. "You'll know in plenty of time, and he's a cinch."

"And nobody knows a thing about him," said McManus.

"Good reason why," laughed Porter. "That's a pretty smart trick: working him away from the track."

"It's the only thing to do," said Johnson. "Zanzibar is a nervous colt, and if I worked him on the track with the other horses he'd go all to pieces. That's why I have Dutchy take him out on a country road and canter him. It keeps him from fretting before a race."

"How fast can he step the three-quarters?" asked Wilson.

"Fast enough to run shoes off of anything around here," said Johnson. "You needn't worry about that. We won't have to put him up against the best, though. Zanzibar didn't do anything last season, and he's bound to get a price in almost any kind of a race."

"You're sure he's under cover?"

"If he ain't under cover, a horse never was. He gets his work before sunrise, and at that most of it is just cantering. I've set him down, though, and I know what he can do."

"It sounds all right," admitted McManus.

"Where do we bet this money?" demanded Porter.

Johnson laughed. "That's a fool question! The less he's played at the track the better. We'll unload in the pool rooms on the Coast, same as we did before. Wilson here can enter Blitzen in the same race, and they can't get away from making Blitzen the favourite: on form they'd have to pick him to win easy.

I'll let it leak out that I'm only sending Zanzibar for a workout and to see whether he's improved any over last season. The pool rooms won't know what hit 'em."

"Hold on!" said McManus suddenly. "Suppose Curry gets into the race."

"Bonehead!" growled Wilson. "You've got Curry on the brain. Outside of Elisha there's no class to his string of beetles, and Elisha is a distance horse. Three-quarters is too short for him."

"He can't get going under half a mile!" supplemented Porter.

"Well," apologised McManus, "I like to figure all the angles."…

Old Man Curry also liked to figure all the angles. He had the utmost confidence in Solomon's statement concerning the righteous man and the seven falls, but this did not keep him from taking the ordinary precautions when preparing for the eighth start and the promised rising up. He knew that the big rawboned bay horse Elijah was a vastly improved animal, but he also desired to know the company in which Elijah would find himself the next time out. His investigations, while inconspicuous were thorough, and soon brought him in contact with the name of an equine stranger.

"Zanzibar, eh?" thought the old man as he left the office of the racing secretary. "Zanzibar? And Johnson owns him. H'm-m. I'll have to find out about that one, sure. The others don't amount to much. But this Zanzibar? If I only had Frank now!"

Since the Bald-faced Kid's retirement from the turf the Curry secret-service department had consisted of Shanghai and Mose, and there were times when the shambling hostler could be much wiser than he looked. It was Shanghai who drew the assignment.

"Boy," said Old Man Curry, "Johnson has got a colt named Zanzibar that starts next Saturday. I thought I knew all the hosses in train-in' round here, but I've overlooked this one. Find out all you can 'bout him."

"Yes, suh!" answered Shanghai. "Bes' way to do that would be to bus' into a crap game. Misteh Johnson got a couple cullud swipes whut might know somethin'—crap-shootin' fools, both of 'em—an' whiles I'm rollin' them bones I could jus' let a few questions slip out. Yes, suh, that's good way, but when you ain't shoot-in' yo' money in the game they jus' nachelly don' know you 'mong them present. If you got couple nice, big, moon-face' dollahs to inves', they can't he'p but notice you. They got to do it!"

Old Man Curry smiled and dipped two fingers and a thumb into his vest pocket.

"*Thank* you, suh!" chuckled Shanghai, trying hard to appear surprised. "Thank you! This sutny goin' *com*bine business with pleasuah!"

"Get away with you!" scolded Old Man Curry.

Now, nearly every one knows that the simon-pure feed-box information, the low-down and the dead-level tip, may be picked up behind any barn where hostlers, exercise boys, and apprentice jockeys congregate. Tongues are loosened at such a gathering, and the carefully guarded secrets of trainers and owners are in danger, for the one absorbing topic of conversation is horse, and then more horse.

Shanghai knew exactly where to go, and departed on his mission whistling jubilantly and chinking two silver dollars in his pocket.

At the end of three hours he returned, his hamlike hands thrust deep into empty pockets, and the look in his eye of one who has watched rosy dreams vanish.

"Where you been all this time?" snapped his employer wrathfully. "'As vinegar to the teeth, and as smoke to the eyes, so is a sluggard to them that send him.' I declare, Solomon must have had some black stable boys! What you been at, you triflin' hound?"

Shanghai smiled a sorrowful smile and shook his head.

"Well, you see, kunnel"—Shanghai always gave his employer a high military rank when in fear of rebuke—"you see, kunnel, it took 'em longer'n usual to break me this mawnin'. I start' off right good, but I sutny bowed a tendon an' pulled up lame. Once I toss six passes at them gamblehs———"

"Never mind that! What did you find out about Zanzibar?"

"Oh, him!" Shanghai blinked rapidly as if dispelling a vision. "Zanzibar? Why, kunnel, they aimin' to slip him oveh Satu'day."

"Ah, hah!" Old Man Curry tugged at his white beard. "Ah, hah. I thought so. Had him under cover, eh? Where have they been workin' him?"

"Out on the county road 'bout two miles f'um yere. You know that nice stretch with all them trees? Every mawnin', early, they takes him out———"

"*Who* takes him out?"

"Li'l white boy they calls Dutchy."

"Nobody else goes with him?"

Shanghai shook his head.

"How old is this boy?" asked the canny horseman.

"How ole? Why, kunnel, I reckon he's risin' fifteen, mebbe."

"Smart boy?"

Shanghai cackled derisively.

"I loaned him a two-bit piece, kunnel, an' he tol' me all he knowed!"

Old Man Curry fell to combing his beard, and Shanghai retreated to the tackle-room where he found Little Mose.

"The boss, he pullin' his whiskehs an' cookin' up a job on somebody," remarked the hostler.

"Huh!" grunted Mose. "It's time he 'uz doin' somethin'! Betteh not leave it *all* to Sol'mun!"

The cooking process lasted until evening, by which time Old Man Curry had ceased to comb his beard and was rolling a straw reflectively from one corner of his mouth to the other.

"You, Shanghai!"

"Yes, suh! Comin' up!"

"Find that little rascal Mose and tell him I want to see him."

"Yes, suh."

"And, Shanghai?"

"Yes, suh."

"I believe I've found the way to rise up!"

"Good news!" ejaculated the startled negro, backing away. But to himself the hostler said: "*Rise up?* Sweet lan' o' libuhty! I wondeh whut bitin' the ole man now?"

It was a small and very sleepy exercise boy whom Smiley Johnson tossed into the saddle at four o'clock on Saturday morning: a boy whose teeth were chattering, for he was cold.

"Canter him the usual distance, Dutchy," said the owner. "Then set him down, but not for more than half a mile. Understand?"

"Y-yes, sir," stammered the boy, rubbing his eyes with the back of one hand.

"Don't let him get hot, now!"

"No, sir; I won't."

"All right. Take him away!"

Johnson slapped Zanzibar on the shoulder, and the colt moved off in the gloom. His rider, whose other name was Herman Getz, huddled himself in the saddle and reflected on several things, including the hard life of an exercise boy, the perils of the dark, and the hot cup of coffee which he would get on his return.

Wrapped in these meditations, he had travelled some distance before he became aware of a dark shape in the road ahead. Coming closer, Herman saw that it was a horse and rider, evidently waiting for him.

"Howdy, Jockey Walsh!" called a voice.

The shortest cut to an exercise boy's heart is to address him as Jockey. Herman's heart warmed toward this stranger, and he drew alongside, trying to make out his features in the darkness.

"'Taint Walsh," said Herman, not without regret. "It's Getz."

"Jockey Getz? I don' seem to place you, jock. Where you been ridin'? East?"

"I ain't a jock. I'm only gallopin' 'em. Who are you?"

"Jockey Jones, whut rides faw Misteh Curry. If you ain't a jock, you sutny ought to be. You don't set a hawss like no exercise boy. Thass why I mistook you faw Walsh."

"What horse is that?"

"This jus' one 'em Curry beetles. Whut you got, jock?"

"Zanzibar."

"Any good?"

"Well," was the cautious reply, "he ain't done anything yet."

The boys jogged on for some time in silence. "You sutny set him nice an' easy," commented Mose. "Le's breeze 'em a little an' see how you handle a hawss." Mose booted his mount in the ribs, chirruped twice, and the horse broke into a gallop. Herman immediately followed suit, and soon the riders were knee to knee, flying along the lonely road.

"Shake him up, jock!" urged Little Mose. "That all you kin get out of him? Shake him up, if you knows how!"

Of course Herman could not allow any one to hint that he did not know how. He went out on Zanzibar's neck and shook him up vigorously, à la Tod Sloan in his palmy days. The colt began to draw ahead. From the rear came shrill encouragement.

"Thass whut I calls reg'luh race ridin', jock! Let him out if he got some lef'!

Let him out!"

Carried away by these kind words, Herman forgot his instructions: forgot everything but the thrill of the race. He drove his heels into Zanzibar's sides and crouched low in the saddle. The cold dawn wind cut like a knife. After a time there came a wail from the rear.

"Nothin' to it, jock! You too good! Too good! Wait faw me."

Herman drew rein, and soon Mose was alongside again. "Canter 'em a while now," said he. "Say, who taught you to ride like that?"

"Nobody," answered Herman modestly. "I just picked it up."

"A natchel-bawn race rideh. Sometimes you finds 'em. I wish't I could set a hawss down like that. Show me again."

"It's easy," bragged Herman, and proceeded to demonstrate that statement. Again the compliments floated from the rear, coupled with requests for speed, and yet more speed. Mose was not an apt pupil, however, for he required a third lesson, and at the end of it Zanzibar was blowing heavily. Mose suggested that they turn and go back. "If I could git that much out of a hawss, I wouldn't take off my cap to no jock!" said he. "Whyn't you make Johnson give you a mount once in a while?"

"He says I ain't smart enough," was the sulky reply.

Little Mose laughed. "He jus' pig-headed, thass all ail him! You like to git a reg'luh job ridin' faw a good man?"

"*Would* I!"

"Well, I knows a man whut wants a good boy. See that tree yondch? That big one? Le's see who kin get there first!"

"It—it's pretty far, ain't it?"

"Shucks! Quahteh of a mile, mebbe. Come on!"

But it was nearer half a mile, and the three brisk sprints had told on the colt. Boot him never so hard, it was all Herman could do to keep Zanzibar on even terms with Mose's mount.

"You on'y foolin' 'ith me. He kin do betteh than that! We in the stretch now; *shake him up!*"

Zanzibar was shaken up for the fourth and last time—shaken up to the limit— and Mose was generous enough to say that the race was a dead heat.

As the boys brought the horses to a walk, another negro stepped out from behind a tree, a blanket on his arm. Mose slipped from the saddle and tossed the bridle to Shanghai.

"Ain't you goin' to ride back to the track?" demanded Herman.

"No. My boss, he always wants this skate blanketed an' led round a while…. Sufferin' mackerel, jock! What you goin' do 'ith that hawss? Shave him?"

Then for the first time Herman realised that Zanzibar was lathered with sweat; for the first time also he recalled his instructions.

"I can't take him back like that!" he cried. "Johnson'll kill me! He told me not to get this horse hot: and look at him!"

"He sutny some *warm*," said Shanghai critically. "He steamin' like a kettle!"

"Whut if he is?" asked Mose. "We kin fix that all hunky-dory, an' Johnson, he won't neveh know."

"How can we fix it?"

"Got to let that sweat dry first," warned Shanghai.

"And then wipe it off," said Mose.

"It comes off easy when it's dry," supplemented Shanghai as he started down the road with the other horse.

"Let him stand a while," said Mose. "We'll tie him up to this tree. Pity you ain't ridin' some 'em races Johnson's jock tosses off. Once round that limb's enough. He'll stand."

And for rather more than half an hour the good colt Zanzibar shivered in a cold wind while Herman warmed himself in the genial glow of flattering speeches and honeyed compliments.

"He looks dry now," said Mose at length. "We'll rub him down with grass. See how easy it comes off an' don't leave no marks neither. Mebbe you betteh not say anythin' to yo' boss 'bout this."

"Say, you don't think I'm a fool, do you?"

"Sutny not! I see yo' a pretty wise kid, all right!"

"If I could only get that reg'lar job you was talkin' about!"

"It boun' to come, jock, boun' to come! You be steerin' 'em down 'at ol' stretch one of these days, sure! If we jus' had a li'l wateh, now, we could do a betteh job on 'is hawss."

"He's shakin' a lot, ain't he?" asked Herman.

"Nuhvous, thass all ail him. My side 'mos' clean a'ready; how you gettin' along?"

Smiley Johnson stood at the entrance to his paddock stall shaking hands with acquaintances, slapping his friends on the back, and passing out information. "I don't know a great deal about this horse," he would remark confidently. "He wasn't much account last season—too nervous and high-strung. I'm only sending him to-day to see what he'll do, but of course he never figured to beat horses like Blitzen. Not enough class."

Curly McManus forced his way into Zanzibar's stall and moved to the far corner where Johnson followed him.

"Curry is in the betting ring," McManus whispered.

"Well, what of that?"

"He's betting an awful chunk of dough on Elijah; they're giving him 4 and 5 to 1."

"The more he bets the more he'll lose."

"But it ain't like him to unbelt for a chunk unless he *knows* something."

Johnson chuckled.

"Most of his betting is done in books where I've got an interest. D'you think they'd be laying top prices on Elijah if they didn't know something too?"

"I guess that's right, Smiley. You didn't warm this one up to-day. Why?"

"It would make him too nervous: the crowd, and all."

"He's fit, is he?"

"Fitter than a snake! We're getting 8 and 10 to 1 in the pool rooms all over the Coast, and I wish we'd gone even stronger with him. Here comes Curry now. Listen to me kid him!"

The old man entered the paddock from the betting ring, bound for Elijah's stall. Johnson halted him with a shout. "Well, old Stick-in-the-mud! You trying to-day?"

"I'm always tryin'," answered Curry mildly. "My hosses are always tryin' too."

"Wish you a lot of luck!"

"Same to you, sir; same to you."

"But everybody can't win."

"True as gospel. I found that out right here at this track."

Old Man Curry continued on his way as calm and untroubled as if his pockets were not loaded down with pasteboards calling for a small fortune in the event of Elijah's winning the race. His instructions to Little Mose were brief:

"Get away in front and stay there."

A few moments later Johnson and McManus leaned over the top rail of the fence and watched the horses on their way to the post.

"That colt of yours looks a little stiff to me," said McManus critically.

"Nonsense! He may be a bit nervous, but he ain't stiff."

"Well, I *hope* he ain't. Curry's horse looks good."

Later they levelled their field glasses at the starting point. Johnson could see nothing but his own colours: a blazing cherry jacket and cap; McManus spent his time watching Little Mose and Elijah.

"Smiley, that nigger is playing for a running start."

"Let him have it. Zanzibar'll be in front in ten jumps. Hennessey knows just how to handle the colt, and he's chain lightning on the break."

"I suppose the boy on Blitzen'll take care of the nigger if he has to. Slats gave him orders. *They're off!*"

Johnson opened his mouth to say something, but the words died away into a choking gurgle. Instead of rushing to the front, the cherry jacket was rapidly dropping back. It was McManus who broke the stunned silence.

"In front in ten jumps, hey? He's *last* in ten jumps, that's what he is: stiffer'n a board! And look where Curry's nigger is, will you?"

"To hell with Curry's nigger!" barked Johnson. "Look at the colt! He—he can't untrack himself: runs like he was all bound up somehow! Something has gone wrong, sure!"

"You bet it has!" snarled McManus. "Quite a pile of dough has gone wrong, and some of it was mine too!"

A comfortable ten lengths to the good at the upper turn, Little Mose addressed a few vigorous remarks to his mount.

"This a nice place faw us to stay, 'Lijah! Them Irish boys all behin' us! Nobody goin' bump you to-day! Nobody goin' slash you 'ith no whip! Go on, big red hawss! Show 'em how we risin' up!"

"The nigger'll win in a romp!" announced McManus disgustedly.

"Oh, dry up! I want to know what's happened to Zanzibar!"

"I can tell you what's *going* to happen to him," remarked the unfeeling McManus. "He's going to finish last, and a damn bad last at that. Why, he can't get up a gallop! Didn't you know any more than to start a horse in that condition?"

"But how the devil did he get stiff all at once?" howled Johnson.

"That's what you'd better find out. How do we know you didn't cross us, Johnson? It would be just like you!"

Old Man Curry, watching at the paddock gate, thrust his hands under the tails of his rusty frock coat and smiled.

"'A just man falleth seven times and riseth up again!'" he quoted softly. "And the wicked: well, they'll have a mighty lame hoss on their hands, I reckon."

Mose began checking Elijah, several lengths in front of the wire.

"Don't go bustin' a lung, hawss," said he. "Might need it again. You winnin' by a mile. A-a-a mile. Sol'mun was right, but maybe he wouldn't have been if I hadn't done some risin' up myse'f this mawnin'! Whoa, hawss! This where they pay off! We th'oo faw the day!"

Old Man Curry was striding down the track from the judges' stand when he met a large man whose face was purple and his language purple also.

"Man, don't talk like that!" said Curry reprovingly. "And ca'm down or you'll bust an artery. You can't win *all* the time: that's what you told me."

Johnson sputtered like a damp Roman candle, but a portion of his remarks were intelligible.

"Oh, Zanzibar?" said Old Man Curry. "He's a right nice colt. He ought to be. He pretty nigh run the legs off my 'Lisha this mornin'."

"Wha—*what's that?*"

"Yes," continued Old Man Curry, "they had it back an' forth up that road, hot an' heavy. I expect maybe Zanzibar got a chill from sweatin' so hard."

Out of the whirl of Mr. Johnson's remarks and statements of intention Curry selected one.

"No," said he, "I reckon you won't beat that German kid to death. He didn't know any better. You won't lay a finger on him, because why? He's on a railroad train by now, goin' home to Cincinnati. I reckoned his mother might like to see him. And you ain't goin' to make no trouble for me, Johnson. Not a mite. You might whip a little kid, you big, bulldozin' windbag, but I reckon you won't stand up to a man, no matter how old he is!"

“I—I’ll have your entries refused!”

“Don’t go to no such trouble as that,” was the soothing reply. “There won’t be no more Curry entries at this track. A just man might fall down seven times again in such a nest of thieves an’ robbers! Tell that to your judges, an’ be damned!”

And, head erect, shoulders squared, and eyes flashing, Old Man Curry started for the betting ring to collect his due.

EGYPTIAN CORN

"Well, you great big hammer-headed lobster, what have you got to say for yourself, eh? *Don't* stand there and look wise when I'm talking to you! Ain't there a race in this country long enough for you to win? A mile and a half ought to give you a chance to open up and step, but what do you do? You come last, just beginning to warm up and go some! Sometimes I think I ought to sell you to a soap factory, you clumsy false alarm, you ugly old fraud, you cross between a mud turtle and a carpenter's bench, you——"

At this point Slim Kern became extremely personal, speaking his mind concerning the horse Pharaoh, his morals, his habits, and his ancestors. Some of his statements would have raised blisters on a salamander, but Pharaoh listened calmly and with grave dignity.

Pharaoh was not handsome. He was, as Slim had said, a hammer-headed brute of imposing proportions. But for his eyes no turfman would have looked at him twice. They were large, clear, and unusually intelligent; they redeemed his homely face. Without them he would have been called a stupid horse.

An elderly gentleman sat on a bale of hay and listened to Slim's peroration. As it grew in power and potency the listener ceased to chew his straw and began to shake his head. When Slim paused for breath, searching his mind for searing adjectives, a mild voice took advantage of the silence.

"There now, Slim, ain't you said enough to him? Seems like, if it was me, I wouldn't cuss a hoss so strong—not *this* hoss anyway. He ain't no fool. Chances are he knows more'n you give him credit for. Some hosses don't care what you say to 'em—goes in one ear and out the other—but Pharaoh, he's wise. He knows that ain't love talk. He's chewin' it over in his mind right now. By the look in his eye, he's askin' himself will he bite your ear off or only kick you into the middle of next week. Cussin' a hoss like that won't make him win races where he never had a chance nohow."

"I know it," said Slim. "I know it, Curry, but think what a wonderful relief it is to me! Take a slant at him, standing there all dignified up like a United States senator! Don't he look like he ought to know something? Wouldn't you think he'd know where they pay off? He makes me sore, and I've just got to talk to him. I've owned him a whole year, and what has he done? Won once at a mile and a quarter, and he'd have been last that time if the leaders hadn't got in a jam on the turn and fell down. He was so far behind 'em when they piled up that all he had to do was pull wide and come on home! He had sense enough for that. I've started him in all the distance races on this circuit; he always runs three feet to their one at the finish, but he's never close enough up to make it count. He must have some notion that they pay off the second time around, and it's all my boy can do to stop him after he goes under the wire. Why won't he uncork some of that stuff where it will get us something? Why won't he? I don't know, and that's what gets me."

Old Man Curry rose, threw away his straw, and circled the horse three times, muttering to himself. This was purely an exhibition of strategy, for Curry knew all about Pharaoh: had known all about him for months.

"What'll you take for him?" The question came so suddenly that it caught Slim off his balance.

"Take for him!" he ejaculated. "Who wants an old hammer-head like that?"

"I was thinkin' I might buy him," was the quiet reply, "if the price is right. I dunno's a hoss named Pharaoh would fit in with a stable of Hebrew prophets, 'count of the way Pharaoh used Moses and the Isrulites, but I might take a chance on him—if the price is right."

Now, Slim would have traded Pharaoh for a nose bag or a sack of shorts and reckoned the intake pure gain, but he was a horseman, and it naturally follows that he was a trader.

"Well, now," said he, "I hadn't thought of selling him, Curry, and that's a fact."

"Did anybody but me ever think of buyin' him?" asked the old man innocently.

"He's got a wonderful breeding," said Slim, ignoring the question. "Yes, sir; he's out of the purple, sure enough, and as for age he's just in his *prime*. There's a lot of racing in him yet. Make me an offer."

"You don't want me to talk first, do you? I don't reckon I could make a real offer on a hoss that never wins 'less all the others fall down. Pharaoh ain't what you might call a first-class buy. From his looks it costs a lot to keep him."

"Not near as much as you'd think," was the quick rejoinder. "Pharaoh's a dainty feeder."

"Ah, hah," said Old Man Curry, stroking his beard. "About as dainty as one of them perpetual hay presses! That nigh foreleg of his has been stove up pretty bad too. How he runs on it at all beats me."

"He's sound as a nut!" declared Slim vehemently. "There ain't a thing in the world the matter with him. Ask any vet to look him over!"

"Well, Slim, I dunno's he's worth the expense. Come on, now; tell me what's the least you'll take for him?"

"Five hundred dollars."

"Give you a hundred and fifty cash."

"Say, do you want me to make you a present of him?" demanded Slim, indignantly sarcastic. "Maybe you think I'd ought to throw in a halter so's you can lead him away!"

"No," said Old Man Curry. "I won't insist on a halter. I got plenty of my own. You said yourself he wa'n't no good and I thought you meant it. I was just askin' if you'd sell him; that was all. Keep him till Judgment Day, if you want him. No harm done." Old Man Curry began to walk away.

"Hold on a minute!" said Slim, trying hard to keep the anxious note out of his voice. "Be reasonable, old-timer. Make me an offer for the horse: one that a sensible man can accept."

Old Man Curry paused and glanced over his shoulder.

"Why," said he, faintly surprised, "I kind of thought I'd done that a'ready!"

"*Look* at him!" urged Slim. "Did you ever see a more powerful horse in your life? And smart too. A hundred and fifty dollars! One side of him is worth more than that!"

"Likely it is," agreed the old man solemnly. "Seems to me I saw a piece in the paper 'bout a cannery where they was goin' to put up hoss-flesh!"

"I admit he's had a lot of bad luck," persisted Slim, "but get Pharaoh warmed up once and he'll surprise you. Didn't you see how fast he was coming to-day?"

"The numbers was up before he got in," was the dry response. "What's the good of a hoss that won't begin to run until the race is over? You said yourself he only won for you when all the others fell down. It's kind of difficult to frame up races that way. Jockeys hate to take the chances. Will two hundred buy him? Two hundred, right in your hand?"

"Oh, come over here and set down!" said Slim. "You ain't in any hurry, are you? Nothing you've said yet interests me. On the level, you ain't got a suspicion of what a good horse this is!"

"No, but I kind of suspicion what a bad hoss he is." Old Man Curry resumed his seat on the bale of hay and produced his packet of fine-cut tobacco. "You tell me how good he is," said he, "and I'll listen, but before you open up here's what Solomon says: 'The simple believeth every word, but the prudent man looketh well to his going.' Hoss tradin' is no job for a simple man, but I made a livin' at it before you was born. Now fire away, and don't tell me this Pharaoh is a gift. 'Whoso boasteth himself of a false gift is like clouds and wind without rain.' I reckon Solomon meant mostly wind. Now you can cut loose an' tell me how much hoss this is."

Two hours later Old Man Curry arrived at his barn leading Pharaoh. He had acquired the hammer-head for the sum of $265 and Slim had thrown in the halter. Shanghai, Curry's hostler and handy man, stared at the new member of the racing string with open-mouthed and pop-eyed amazement.

"Lawd's sake! What *is* that, a cam-u-el?"

"No, I don't reckon he's a camel, exactly," replied the old man. "I don't know just what he is, Shanghai, but I'm aimin' to find out soon. The man I got him from allowed as he was a race hoss."

"Huh-uh, kunnel! He sutny don' ree'semble no runnin' hawss to *me*. I neveh yet see a head shape' like that on anything whut could run." Shanghai came closer and examined the equine stranger carefully. "Yo' an ugly brute, big hawss: ugly no name faw it. Oh-oh, kunnel; he got a knowin' eye, ain't he? If this hawss is wise as he look, he ought to be a judge in the Soopreme Cote! Yes, suh; somepin' besides bone in that ole hammeh-head!"

"I bought him for his eyes," said Old Man Curry. "His eyes and his name. This is Pharaoh, Shanghai."

"Faro, eh?" The negro chuckled. "Thass a game where yo' gits action two ways: bet it is or it ain't. Now, mebbe this yere Faro is a race hawss, an' mebbe he ain't, but if yo' eveh puts him in with early speed an' a short distance to go, betteh play him with a copper, kunnel. He got same chance as a eagle flyin' a mile 'gainst pigeons."

"The thing to do," said Old Man Curry with his kindly smile, "is to find out the eagle's distance."

Little Mose was dreaming that he had piloted the winner of the Burns Handicap and was being carried to the jockey's room in a floral horseshoe which rocked in a very violent manner. The motion became so pronounced that Mose opened his eyes, and found Old Man Curry shaking him.

"Get up, you lazy little rascal! Got a job for you this mornin'. Turn out!"

The jockey sat up, yawning and knuckling his eyes.

"Solomon must have had at least one little black boy," said the old man. "'Love not sleep lest thou come to poverty.' Hurry up, Mose!"

"Yes, suh," mumbled the drowsy youngster. "Reckon Sol'mun neveh had to gallop a string an' ride 'em too. I sutny earns whut I gits when I git it."

Dawn was breaking when Jockey Moseby Jones emerged from the tack room to find Old Man Curry and Pharaoh waiting for him. As they were walking to the track the owner gave his orders.

"One trouble with this hoss," said he, "is that the boy who has been ridin' him wasn't strong enough in the arms to keep his head up."

"That ol' hawss has got a head whut weighs a thousan' pounds!" murmured Mose sulkily. "'Spect he'll 'bout yank both arms outen me!"

"You're pretty stout for a boy your size," said the old man, "an' you may be able to hold this big, hard-stridin' hoss together an' shake something out of him. Send him two miles, Mose, keep his head up if you can, an' ride him every jump of the way."

"But, boss, they ain't no two-mile races in thisyer part o' the country!"

"Keep on, an' you'll talk yourself into a raw-hidin' yet, little black boy. I ain't askin' you to tell me 'bout the races on the jungle tracks. All you got to think about is can you handle as much hoss as this over a distance of ground. If you can, an' he's got the stayin' qualities I think he has, you an' me an' Pharaoh may go on a long journey—down into Egypt after corn. Git up on him, Mose, an' let's see what you both can do."

The hammer-head loafed away at a comfortable stride and his first mile showed nothing, but his second circuit of the track was a revelation which caused Old Man Curry to address remarks to his stop watch. It took every ounce of Mose's strength to fight Pharaoh to a standstill: the big brute was just beginning to enjoy the exercise and wanted to keep on going.

"Well, think you can handle him?"

"Boss," panted little Mose, "I kin do—everything to thisyer hoss—but stop him. He sutny—do love to run—once he git goin'. All the way—down the stretch—he was asayin' to me: 'Come on, jock! Lemme go round again!' Yes, suh, he was beggin' me faw 'notheh mile!"

"Ah-hah," said Old Man Curry. "That's the way it looked to me. Well, tomorrow we'll let him do that extra mile, but we'll get up earlier. By an' by when he's ready, we'll let him run four miles an' see how he finishes an' what the watch says."

Little Mose rolled his eyes thoughtfully.

"Seem like I ain't heard tell of but *one* fo' mile race," he hinted. "'Tain't run in Egypt neitheh. They runs it down round 'Frisco. The Thawntum Stakes is whut they calls it. Boss, you reckon Pharaoh kin pick up any corn in

California?"

Old Man Curry's eyes twinkled, but his voice was stern.

"If I was a little black boy," said he, "an' I was wantin' my boss to take me on a trip down into Egypt, I wouldn't call it California. If I knew anything 'bout a four-mile stake race, I'd try to mislay the name of it. If I had been ridin' a big, hammer-headed hoss, I don't think I'd mention him except in my prayers. If I was goin' after corn, I don't believe I'd say so."

Mose listened, nodding from time to time.

"Boss," said he earnestly, "I sutny always did want to see whut thisyer Egypt looks like. Outside of that, I neveh heard nothin', I don't know nothin', an' I can't tell nothin'. Beginnin' now, a clam has got me beat in a talkin' match!"

Old Man Curry smiled and combed his long, white beard.

"That is the very best way," said he, "to earn a trip down into Egypt. 'A talebearer revealeth secrets, but he that is of a faithful spirit concealeth the matter.'"

"Thass me all oveh!" chuckled Mose. "I bet I got the faithfulest an' the concealin'est spirit whut is!"

Port Costa is a small town on the Carquinez Straits, that narrow ribbon of wind-swept water between San Pablo and Suisun Bays. The early empire builders, striving to reach the Pacific by rail, found it necessary to cross the Carquinez Straits, and to that end built a huge ferryboat capable of swallowing up long overland trains. It was then that Port Costa came into being: a huddle of hastily constructed frame saloons along the water front and very little else. All day and all night the big ferryboat plied between Benicia and Port Costa, transferring rolling stock. While the trains were being made up on the Port Costa side passengers in need of liquid sustenance paid visits to the saloons. They got exactly what the transient may expect in any country.

Henry Ashbaugh sat at a table in Martin Dugan's place and eyed the bartender truculently. He had purchased nothing, for the most excellent of reasons, but he had patronised the free lunch extensively.

"You don't need to look at me like that," said Henry when the silence became unbearable. "I'm waiting for a friend and when he comes he'll buy."

At this critical juncture the swinging doors opened to admit the friend, a tall, elderly man with a patriarchal white beard, clad in a battered black slouch hat and a venerable frock coat. Ashbaugh jumped up with a yell.

"Well, you old son of a gun! It's good for sore eyes to see you! How long has it been, eh?"

"Quite some years," answered Old Man Curry, allowing himself to be guided to the bar. "And how's the world been usin' you, Henry?"

"It's been using me rough, awful rough," replied Ashbaugh. "I ain't even got the price of a drink."

Curry laid a silver coin upon the bar.

"Have one with me," said he.

"Don't mind if I do," said Ashbaugh, and poured out a stiff libation of water-front whisky. Old Man Curry took water, and the wise bartender, after one look at the stranger, drew it from a faucet.

"How!" said Henry, tilting the poison into his system.

"My regards!" said Old Man Curry, sipping his water slowly.

"Same old bird!" ejaculated Ashbaugh, clapping Curry on the back. "Solomon on the brain! Speaking of birds, though, did you ever see one that could fly with only one wing?"

"I never did," was the grave response. "Have another?"

"If you force me," said Ashbaugh, pouring out a second heavy dose. Old Man Curry took more water. Ashbaugh gulped once and passed the back of his hand over his lips.

"We have talked of birds," said he, wheedlingly. "Leave us now talk of centipedes."

"No," said Curry quietly. "No, I reckon not, Henry. There's something else to talk about. You got my telegram?"

"This afternoon," said Ashbaugh with a lingering glance at the bottle. "That's why I'm here."

"You've still got your place out on the Martinez road?" asked Old Man Curry.

"I can't get rid of it," was the answer.

"I'd like to take a hoss down there and put him up for a few weeks, Henry."

"The place is all yours!" said Ashbaugh with wide gestures. "All yours! A friend of mine can have anything I've got, and no questions asked. Where is this here horse?"

"They'll be takin' him out of a freight car about now," said Curry. "Could I git him down to your place to-night?"

"You can if you walk it."

"Is the road as good as it used to be?"

"Same road. Just like it was when you used to train horses on it."

"Mebbe we ought to be going," suggested Old Man Curry.

"Then you won't talk about centipedes?"

"Oh, well," smiled the old man, "I might discuss a three-legged critter with you—once."

"Put that bottle back on the bar!" said Ashbaugh.

The overnight entry slips, given out on the day before the running of the Thornton Stakes, bore the name of the horse Pharaoh, together with that of his owner, C. T. Curry, whereat the wise men of the West chuckled. A few of them had heard of Old Man Curry, a queer, harmless individual who owned bad horses and raced them on worse tracks. A hasty survey of turf guides brought the horse Pharaoh to unfavourable light as a nonwinner in cheap company, and in no sense to be considered as a competitor in the second greatest of Western turf classics. In addition to this, those who made it their business to know the business of horsemen were able to state positively that no such horse as Pharaoh had arrived at the Emeryville track outside of Oakland. Consequently, when the figuring was done (and a great deal of figuring is always done on the eve of an important stake race), the Curry entry was regarded as among the scratches.

On paper, the rich purse was a gift to the imported mare Auckland. Australian horses, bred to go a distance, had often won this longest of American stakes, and Auckland was known to be one of the very best animals ever brought across the Pacific. It was only a question of how far she would win, and the others were considered as competing for second and third money. On the night before the race all the talk was of Auckland; all the speculation had to do with her price, and how many dollars a man might have to bet to win one. At noon on the day of the race a horse car was shunted in on one of the spur tracks at Emeryville, and a group of idlers gathered to watch the unloading process. No little amusement was afforded them by the appearance and costume of the owner, but Old Man Curry paid not the slightest attention to the half-audible comment, and soon the "Bible horses" found their feet on the ground once more.

Among the loafers were some "outside men" employed by the bookmakers, and these endeavoured to acquire information from Old Man Curry, without success. The negro Shanghai proved more loquacious. He trudged at the end of the line leading a big hammer-headed brute which he often addressed as "Faro."

"Who owns these hawsses?" repeated Shanghai. "Mist' Curry—thass him in front—he owns 'em. We got here jus' in time, I reckon. Thisyer hawss whut I'm leadin', he goes in that Thawntum Stakes to-day."

"Nix!" said the outside man. "Just off the cars, and he's going to start? It can't be done!"

"I ain't heard the boss say he'd scratch him," said Shanghai.

"But how long have you been on the way?"

"Oh, I reckon 'bout five days. Yes, suh; we been exackly five days *an'* nights gettin' here."

"Then you're kidding about that horse going to start in the Thornton Stakes."

"No, suh; I ain't kiddin' nobody. Thass whut we brought him oveh faw: to staht him in them Thawntum Stakes. I reckon he'll have to do the bes' he know how."

"Are you going to bet on him?"

"Says *which*?" Shanghai showed a double row of glistening ivories. "No, indeedy! Hawss got to show me befo' I leggo my small change! This Faro, he can't seem to win no mile races, so the boss he thinks he might do betteh in a long one. But me, I ain't bettin' on him, no suh!"

Only five horses faced the barrier in the Thornton Stakes. Second money was not enough of a temptation to the owners, who could see nothing but the Australian mare, Auckland. The opening prices bore out this belief. Auckland was quoted at 1 to 5, a prohibitive figure; Baron Brant, the hope of the California contingent, at 4 to 1; The Maori at 8 to 1; Ambrose Churchill at 12 to 1, and Pharaoh was held at 15 and 20. The bookmakers had heard that the Curry horse had been taken from the car at noon, and wondered at the obstinacy of his owner in starting him, stiff and cramped from a long railroad journey.

"Must be figuring to give him a workout and a race all at once," said the chalk merchants.

All these things being known, a certain elderly gentleman did not have to beg the bookmakers to take his money. He passed from block to block in the big ring, stripping small bills from a fat roll, and receiving pasteboards in exchange. Round and round the ring he went, with his monotonous request:

"Ten on Pharaoh to win, please."

Every bookmaker was glad to oblige him; most of them thanked him for the ten-dollar bills. There were thirty-two books in the circle, and Old Man Curry visited each one of them several times. He stopped betting only when he heard the saddling bell ringing in the paddock. After a few words with Little Mose, he returned to the betting ring and the distribution of his favours.

When the five horses stood at the barrier in front of the grand stand, Pharaoh was conspicuous only for his size and the colour of his rider. The mare Auckland, beautifully proportioned, her smooth coat glistening in the sun, was the ideal racing animal.

The word was soon given, the barrier whizzed into the air, and the five horses were on their long journey. The boy on Auckland sent her to the front at once, and the mare settled into her long, easy stride, close to the rail, saving every possible inch. Pharaoh immediately dropped into last position, plodding through the dust kicked up by the field. The big hammer-head showed nothing in the first mile save dogged persistence. At the end of the second mile Auckland was twenty lengths in front of Pharaoh, and running without effort. The Maori and Ambrose Churchill were beginning to drop back, but Baron Brant still clung to second place, ten lengths behind the favourite.

It was in the third mile that Jockey Moseby Jones began to urge the big horse. At first there seemed to be no result, but gradually, almost imperceptibly, the heavy plugging stride grew longer. Auckland still held her commanding lead, but Pharaoh marked his gain on Ambrose Churchill and The Maori, leaving them a bitter and hopeless battle for fourth place. In the home stretch the pace began to tell on Baron Brant, and he faded. Pharaoh caught and passed him just at the wire, with the Australian mare fifteen lengths in front and eating up the distance in smooth, easy strides.

The stubborn persistence of the hammer-headed horse had not escaped the crowd, and those who support the underdog in an uphill fight gave him a tremendous cheer as he swung down to the turn. It was then that Little Mose leaned forward and began hand-riding, calling on Pharaoh in language sacred and profane.

"Hump yo'self, big hawss! Neveh let it be said that a mare kin make you eat dust! Lay down to it, Faro, lay down to it! Why, you ain't begun to run yit! You jus' been foolin'! You want to show me up befo' a big town crowd! Faro, I ast you from my *heart*, lay down to it!"

And Pharaoh lay down to it. The ugly big brute let himself out to the last notch, hugging the rail with long, ungainly strides. The jockey on Auckland had counted the race as won—in fact, he had been spending the winner's fee from the end of the second mile—but on the upper turn the thud of hoofs came to his ears, and with them wild whoops of encouragement. He looked back over his shoulder in surprise which soon turned to alarm; the big hammer-head was barely six lengths away and drawing nearer with every awkward bound. Jockey McFee sat down on his imported mount and began to ride for a five-thousand-dollar stake, a fat fee, his reputation, and several other considerations, but always he heard the voice of the little negro, coming closer and closer:

"Corn crop 'bout ripe, Faro! Jus' waitin' to be picked! That mare, she come a long ways to git it, but she goin' git it good! Them ribbons don't keep her f'um rockin'; she's all through! Go git her, big hawss! Go git her!"

Jockey McFee slashed desperately with his whip as Pharaoh thundered alongside, and the game mare gave up her last ounce: gave it up in a losing fight. Once, twice, the ugly, heavy head and the head of the equine aristocrat rose and fell side by side; then Auckland dropped back beaten and broken-hearted while her conqueror pounded on to the wire, to win by five open lengths....

At least one dream came true. Moseby Jones was carried off the track in a gorgeous floral horseshoe, his woolly head bobbing among the roses and his teeth putting the white carnations to shame. Shanghai danced all the way from the judges' stand to the stables, not an easy feat when one considers that he was leading the winner of the Thornton Stakes, also garlanded and bedecked within an inch of his life, but, in spite of all his floral decorations, extremely dignified.

Old Man Curry fought his way through a mob of reporters and fair-weather acquaintances to find himself face to face with the only real surprise of the day. A sharp-faced youth, immaculately dressed, leaped upon him, endeavouring to embrace him, shake his hand and congratulate him, all in a breath. "Frank!" cried the old man. "Bless your heart, boy, where did you come from?"

"From Butte," answered the Bald-faced Kid. "Wanted to get some ideas on the spring trade; saw you had a horse in the Thornton Stakes; thought I might find you; got here just as the race finished. Old-timer, how are you? You don't know how good it is to see you again!"

"I know how good it is to see you, my son!" The old man laid his arm across the youth's shoulders. "How's the wife, Frank?"

"Just bully! She would have been here with me, but she couldn't leave the kid: couldn't leave Curry——"

The patriarch of the Jungle Circuit reached hastily for his fine-cut.

"It—it was a boy, then?" he asked.

The Bald-faced Kid grinned.

"Better than that; it was a girl! We had the name picked out in advance. The wife wouldn't have it any other way."

Old Man Curry shook his head solemnly. "Frank," said he, "you know that ain't treat-in' a little girl right! Curry! It sounds like the stuff you eat with rice! When she gits old enough to know she'll hate it, and me, too."

"Any kid of mine is going to *love* the name of Curry, and call you grandpa! What do you think of that? You don't need to worry, and I won't even argue the point with you. My wife says——"

"Anything your wife says is right," interrupted the old man, blowing his nose lustily. "Why, it kind of seems as if I had some folks——"

"If you don't think you've got a ready-made family," said the Kid, "come over to Butte any time and I'll win a bet from you. But I can tell you about that later. What I want to know is this: I met a couple of hustlers here to-day —boys I used to team with—and they told me Pharaoh didn't have a chance because he went right from the box car to the paddock. He gets off the train, where he's been for five days and nights, and comes so close to the American record that there ain't any fun in it. Now, you know that can't be done. Old-timer, you pulled many a miracle on me before I quit the turf; give me an inside on this one!"

Old Man Curry smiled benignantly.

"Well, son, mebbe I kind of took advantage of 'em there."

"It wouldn't be the first time, dad. Let's have it."

"All right. To start with, I bought this hoss for little or nothing. Mostly nothing. I knew he was a freak. He couldn't begin to untrack himself till he had gone a mile, but after that it seemed like every mile he went he got better. I held a watch on him an' he ran four miles close enough to the record to show me that he had a chance in the Thornton Stakes. Five weeks ago I shipped him out to Port Costa an' took him off the train there——"

"Holy Moses!" breathed the Kid. "I begin to get it, but go on!"

"I knew a man there an' he let me train Pharaoh at his place, Little Mose givin' him a gallop every day. That Benicia road is as good as any race track. Then I did some close figgerin' on freight schedules, an' telegraphed Shanghai when to leave with the rest of the stable. They got into Port Costa this mornin'. It wa'n't no trick at all to slip Pharaoh into that through car—not when you know the right people—an' when we unloaded here this noon the word sort of got scattered round that the Curry hosses had been five days on the road. Now, no man with the sense that God gives a goose could figger a critter to walk out of a box car, where he'd been bumped an' jolted an' shook up for five days, an' run four miles with any kind of hosses. It just ain't in the book, son.

"They got the notion I was crazy, an' I reckon they knew everything about us but the one thing that counted most, which was that Pharaoh hadn't been in that car an hour all told. You know, when you go down into Egypt after corn, you got to do as the Egyptians do: have an ace in the hole all the time. Solomon says that a fool uttereth all his mind, but a wise man keepeth it till afterward. That's why I'm gassin' so much now, I reckon."

"Old-timer," chuckled the Kid, "you're a wonder, and I'm proud to have a kid named for you! Just one question more, and I'm through. You won the stake, and that amounts to quite a mess of money, but did you bet enough to pay the freight on the string?"

"Well, now, son," said the old man; "I been so glad to see you that I kind of forgot that part of it." He fumbled in the tail pockets of his rusty black frock coat and brought forth great handfuls of tickets. "I didn't take less'n 15 to 1," said he, "an' I bet 'em till my feet ached, just walkin' from one book to another. I haven't tried to figger it up, but I reckon I took more corn away from these Egyptians than the law allows a single man to have. If it's all the same to you, Frank, an' the baby ain't got no objections, I'd like to use some of this to start a savings account for my namesake. Curry ain't no name for a baby girl, an' you ought to let me square it with her somehow. Mebbe when she gits of age, an' wants to marry some harum-scarum boy, she won't think so bad of her gran'daddy."

THE MODERN JUDGMENT OF SOLOMON

It was an unpleasantly warm morning, and the thick, black shade of an umbrella tree made queer neighbours—as queer neighbours as the Jungle Circuit could produce. Old Man Curry found the shade first and felt that he was entitled to it by right of discovery, consequently he did not move when Henry M. Pitkin signified an intention of sharing the coolness with him. Old Man Curry had less than a bowing acquaintance with Pitkin, wished to know him no better, and had disliked him from the moment he had first seen him.

"Hot, ain't it?" asked the newcomer by way of making a little talk. "What you reading, Curry?"

Old Man Curry looked up from the thirteenth chapter of Proverbs, ceased chewing his straw, and regarded Pitkin with a grave and appraising interest which held something of disapproval, something of insult. Pitkin's eyes shifted.

"It says here," remarked the aged horseman, "'A righteous man hateth lying: but a wicked man is loathsome, and cometh to shame.'"

"Fair enough," said Pitkin, "and serves him right. He ought to come to shame. Pretty hot for this time of year."

"It'll be hotter for some folks by and by."

Pitkin laughed noisily.

"Where do you get that stuff?" he demanded.

"I hope I ain't agoin' to git it," said Old Man Curry. "I aim to live so's to miss it." He lapsed into silence, and the straw began to twitch to the slow grinding motion of his lower jaw. A very stupid man might have seen at a glance that Curry did not wish to be disturbed, but for some reason or other Pitkin felt the need of conversation.

"I've been thinking," said he, "that my racing colours are too plain—yellow jacket, white sleeves, white cap. There's so many yellows and whites that people get 'em mixed up. How would it do if I put a design on the back of the jacket—something that would tell people at a glance that the horse was from the Pitkin stable?"

Old Man Curry closed his book.

"You want 'em to know which is your hosses?" he asked. "Is that the idee?"

"Sure," answered Pitkin. "I was trying to think up a design of some kind.

Lucky Baldwin, used to have a Maltese cross. How would it do if I had a rooster or a rising sun or a crescent sewed on to the back of the jacket?"

Old Man Curry pretended to give serious thought to the problem.

"Roosters an' risin' suns don't mean anything," said he judicially. "An emblem ought to *mean* something to the public—it ought to stand for something."

"Yes," said Pitkin, "but what can I get that will sort of identify me and my horses?"

"Well," said the old man, "mebbe I can suggest a dee-sign that'll fill the bill." He picked up a bit of shingle and drew a pencil from his pocket. "How would this do? Two straight marks this way, Pitkin, an' two straight marks *that* way —and nobody'd ever mistake your hosses—nobody that's been watchin' the way they run."

Pitkin craned his neck and snorted with wrath. Old Man Curry had drawn two crosses side by side, and the inference was plain.

"That's your notion, is it?" said he, rising. "Well, one thing is a mortal cinch, Curry; you'll never catch me psalm singing round a race track, and any time I want to preach, I'll hire a church! Put that in your pipe and smoke it!"

"I ain't smokin', thankee, I'm chewin' mostly," remarked the old gentleman to Pitkin's vanishing coat tails. "Well, now, looks like I made him sort of angry. What is it that Solomon wrote 'bout the anger of a fool?"

They used to say that the meanest man in the world was the Mean Man from Maine, but this is a slander on the good old Pine Tree State, for Henry M. Pitkin never was east of the Mississippi River in his life. He claimed Iowa as his native soil, and all that Iowa could do about it was to issue a warrant for his arrest on a charge connected with the misappropriation of funds. Young Mr. Pitkin escaped over the State line westward, beating the said warrant a nose in a whipping finish, and after a devious career covering many years and many States he turned up on the Jungle Circuit, bringing with him a string of horses, a gentle, soft-spoken old negro trainer, an Irish jockey named Mulligan, and two stable hands, each as black as the ace of spades.

The Jungle Circuit has always been peculiarly rich in catch-as-catch-can burglars and daylight highwaymen, but after they had studied Mr. Pitkin's system closely these gentlemen refused to enter into a protective alliance with him, for, as Grouchy O'Connor remarked, "the sucker hadn't never heard that there ought to be honour among thieves." Pitkin would shear a black sheep as close to the shivering hide as he would shear a white one, and the horses of the Pitkin stable performed according to price, according to investment, according to orders—according to everything in the world but agreement, racing form, and honest endeavour. In ways that are dark and tricks that are vain the heathen Chinee at the top of his heathenish bent would have been no match for Mr. Henry M. Pitkin, who could have taken the shirt away from a Chinese river pirate.

The double-cross would have been an excellent racing trade-mark for the Pitkin stable, because Pitkin had double-crossed every one who ever trusted him, every one with whom he had come in contact. He had even double-crossed old Gabe Johnson, his negro trainer, and the history of that cross will furnish an accurate index on the smallness of Pitkin's soul.

How such a decent old darky as Uncle Gabe ever came to be associated with white trash of the Pitkin variety is another and longer story. It is enough to say that Pitkin hired the old man when he was hungry and thereafter frequently reminded him of that fact. They had been together for three years when they came to the Jungle Circuit—Pitkin rat-eyed, furtive, mysterious as a crow, and scheming always for his own pocket; Uncle Gabe quiet, efficient, inclined to be religious, knowing his place and keeping it and attending strictly to business, namely, the conditioning of the Pitkin horses for the track.

Uncle Gabe treated all white men with scrupulous respect, even touching his hat brim every time Pitkin spoke to him. He was a real trainer of a school fast passing away, and at rare intervals he spoke of the "quality folks down yondeh" for whom he had handled thoroughbreds, glimpses of his history which made his present occupation seem all the stranger by contrast.

Some of the horsemen of the Jungle Circuit pretended to believe that Pitkin kept a negro trainer because he was too mean to get along with a white man, but this was only partly true. He kept Gabe because he had a keen appreciation of the old man's knowledge of horseflesh, and in addition to this Gabe was cheap at the price—fifty dollars a month and his board, and only part of that fifty paid, for it hurt Pitkin to part with money under any circumstances.

It was by skipping pay days that he came to owe Uncle Gabe the not unimportant sum of five hundred dollars, and it was by trying to collect this amount that the aged trainer became also the owner of a race horse.

Pitkin, in the course of business dealings with a small breeding farm, had picked up two bay colts. They were as like as two peas with every honest right to the resemblance, for they were half-brothers by the same sire, and there was barely a week's difference in their ages. Uncle Gabe looked the baby racers over very carefully before giving it as his opinion that no twins were ever more alike in appearance.

"They own mammies would have a li'l trouble tellin' them colts apaht," said the negro.

"Can you tell them apart?" asked Pitkin.

Gabe grinned. "Yes, suh," he answered. "They *is* a difference."

Pitkin looked at Gabe sharply. He knew that the old negro felt one colt to be better than the other.

"All right then," he said after a moment. "Tell you what I'll do. You've been deviling me for that five hundred dollars till I'm sick of listening to you. Take your pick of the two colts and call it square. How does that strike you?"

Uncle Gabe deliberated for some time. The five hundred dollars meant a great deal to him, but the cash value of a debt is regulated somewhat by the sort of man who owes it and Gabe realized that this point was worthy of consideration. On the other hand, should the colt turn out well, he would be worth several times five hundred dollars.

"Don't wait till you get 'em in training," said Pitkin. "A blind man could pick the best one then. Take the colt that looks good to you *now* and let it go at that."

That evening Uncle Gabe made his selection and immediately announced that he intended to name his colt General Duval.

"Good enough," said Pitkin, "and just to carry out the soldier idea, I'll call the other one Sergeant Smith. Put the General in that end stall, away from the others."

The next morning Gabe sent one of the stable hands to get his colt, and when the animal appeared the old trainer's lower lip began to droop, but he said nothing until after he had made a thorough examination. "Boy, you done brought me the wrong colt," said he. "This ain't Gen'al Duval."

"I got him outen yo' stall," said the stable hand.

"Don't care where yo' got him," persisted Gabe. "This ain't the colt I picked out. He ain't wide enough between the eyes."

"What's the argument about?" asked Pitkin, coming from the tackle-room.

"Gabe say thisyer ain't his colt," answered the stable hand.

"Where did you get him?" demanded Pitkin.

"Outen that stall yondeh," said the stable hand, pointing.

"That was where you put your colt, wasn't it?" asked Pitkin, turning to Uncle Gabe.

"Yes, suh, I put him there all right, but this ain't him."

"Oh, come now," laughed Pitkin, "you've been thinking it over and you're afraid you've picked the wrong one. Be a sport, Gabe; stick with your bargain."

"Been some monkey business done round yere," muttered the aged negro. "Been a li'l night walkin', mebbe. Boy, bring out that Sergeant Smith colt an' lemme cas' my eye oveh him once!"

"See here, nigger!" said Pitkin, "I let you have first pick, didn't I? Gave you all the best of it, and you picked this colt here. If you've changed your mind overnight, I can't help that, can I?"

"My mind ain't changed none," replied old Gabe, "but this colt, he's changed, suh."

"Who would change him on you, eh? Do you think *I'd* do it? Is that what you're getting at?"

"Why—why, no suh, no, but——"

"Then shut up! You're always beefing about something or other, always kicking! I don't want to hear any more out of you, understand? Shut up!"

"Yes, suh," answered old Gabe, touching his hat, "all the same I got a right to my opinion, boss."

Whatever his opinion, Gabe proceeded to train the two colts in the usual manner, and before long it was plain to everyone connected with the Pitkin establishment that the striking likeness did not extend to track promise and performance. Sergeant Smith developed into a high-class piece of racing property; General Duval was not worth his oats. Sergeant Smith won some baby races in impressive fashion and was immediately tabbed as a comer and a useful betting tool, but every time General Duval carried the racing colours of Gabriel Johnson—cherry jacket, green sleeves, red, white and blue cap— he brought them home powdered with the dust of defeat.

Old Gabe made several ineffectual attempts to persuade Pitkin to take the colt back again on any terms, and was laughed at for his pains.

"You had your choice, didn't you?" Pitkin would say. "Well, then, you can't blame anybody but yourself. Whose fault is it that I got the good colt and you got the crab? No, Gabe, a bargain's a bargain with me, always. The General's a rotten bad race horse, but he's yours and not mine. It's what you get for being a poor picker."

The bay colts were nearing the end of their three-year-old form when the Pitkin string arrived on the Jungle Circuit and took up quarters next door to

Old Man Curry and his "Bible horses." Sergeant Smith was the star of the stable and the principal money winner, when it suited Pitkin to let him run for the money, while General Duval, as like his half brother as a reflection in a flawless mirror, had a string of defeats to his discredit and his feed bill was breaking old Gabe's heart. The trainer often looked at General Duval and shook his head.

"You an' that otheh colt could tell me somethin' if yo' could *talk*," he frequently remarked.

After his conversation with Old Man Curry, Pitkin returned to his tackle-room in a savage state of mind, and, needing a target for his abuse, selected Mulligan, the Irish jockey.

Now, Mulligan was small, but he had the heart of a giant and the courage of one conviction and two acquittals on charges of assault and battery. In spite of his size—he could ride at ninety-eight pounds—Mulligan was a man in years, a man who felt that his employer had treated him like a child in money matters, and when Pitkin called him a bow-legged little thief and an Irish ape, he was putting a match to a powder magazine.

One retort led to another, and when Mulligan ran out of retorts he responded with a piece of 2 by 4 scantling which he had been saving for just such an emergency, and Pitkin lost interest in the conversation.

Mulligan left him lying on the floor of the tackle-room, and though he was in somewhat of a hurry to be gone he found time to say a few words to old Gabe, who was sunning himself at the end of the barn.

"And I don't know what you can do about it," concluded the jockey, "but anyway I've put you wise. If they ask you, just say that you don't know which way I went."

That night Old Man Curry had a visitor who entered his tackle-room, hat in hand and bowing low.

"Set down, Gabe," said the old horseman. "How's Pitkin by this time?"

"He got a headache," answered Gabe soberly.

"Humph!" snorted Curry. "Should think he would have. That boy fetched him a pretty solid lick. Glad he didn't hurt him any worse—for the boy's sake, I mean."

"Yes, suh," said Gabe. "Mist' Curry, you been mighty good to me, one way'n anotheh, an' I'd like to ast yo' fo' some advice."

"Well," said the old man, "advice is like medicine, Gabe—easy to give but hard to take. What's troublin' you now?"

"Mist' Curry, yo' 'membeh me tellin' yo' 'bout that Gen'al Duval colt of mine —how he neveh did look the same to me since I got him?"

"Yes," answered Curry, "an' I've a'ready told you that you can't prove anything on Pitkin. You may suspect that somebody switched them colts on you, but unless——"

"'Scuse me, suh," interrupted Gabe, "but I got beyon' suspectin' it now. I *knows* it was done."

"You don't say!"

"Yes, suh, I got the proof. Mulligan, he say to me jus' befo' he lights out, 'Gabe,' he say, 'that Smith colt, he belong to you by rights. Pitkin, he pulls a switch afteh yo' went to bed that first night.' He say he seen him do it."

"Mebbe the boy was just tryin' to stir up a little more trouble," suggested Old Man Curry.

"Ain't I tol' you he neveh did *look* the same? Them colts so much alike they had me guessin'. I done picked the one whut was widest between the eyes— an' that's the one whut been awinnin' all them races. That ain't Sergeant Smith at all—that's my Gen'al Duval. Pitkin, he gives me my pick an' then he switches on me. Question is, how kin I git him back?"

Old Man Curry combed his whiskers for some time in silence.

"Solomon had a job like this once," said he, "but it was a question of babies. I reckon his decision wouldn't work out with hosses. Gabe, you're gittin' to be quite an old man, ain't you?"

"Tollable ole," replied the negro; "yes, suh."

"An' if you got this hoss away from Pitkin, what would you do with him?"

"Sell him," was the prompt reply.

"Oho! Then it ain't the hoss you want so much as the money, eh?"

"Mist' Curry, that colt'd fetch enough to sen' me home *right*. I got two sons in Baltimo', an' they been wantin' me to quit the racin' business, but I couldn't quit it broke. No, suh, I couldn't, so I jus' been hangin' on tooth an' toenail like the sayin' is, hopin' I'd git a stake somehow."

"And you don't much care *how* you quit, so long's you quit; is that it?"

"Well, suh, I don't want no trouble if I kin he'p it, but if I has to fight my way loose from Pitkin I'll do it."

There was another long silence while Gabe waited.

"I reckon Solomon would have his hands full straightenin' out this tangle," said Old Man Curry at last. "You can't break into the stall an' take that hoss away from Pitkin, because he'd have you arrested. And then, of course, he's got him registered in his name an' runnin' in his colours—that's another thing we've got to take into consideration. I reckon we better set quiet a few days an' study. You'll know whenever this Sergeant hoss is entered in a race, won't you?"

"Yes, suh; I'm boun' to know ahead o' time, suh."

"All right. Go on back to work an' don't quarrel with Pitkin. Don't let him know that you've found out anything, an' keep me posted on Sergeant Smith. Might be a good thing if we knew when Pitkin is goin' to bet on him. He's been cheatin' with that hoss lately."

"He's always cheatin', suh. Yo'—yo' think they's a way to—to——"

"There's always a way, Gabe," answered Old Man Curry. "The main thing is to find it."

"That's my hoss by right," said the negro, with a trace of stubbornness in his tone.

"An' the world is your oyster," responded Curry, "but you can't go bustin' into it with dynamite. You got to open an oyster, careful. Now go on back to your barn and do as I tell you. Understand?"

"Yes, suh, an' thank yo' kin'ly, suh."

Pitkin's bandaged head brought him little sympathy—in fact, the general opinion seemed to be that Mulligan had not hit him quite hard enough to do the community any good. Certainly the scantling did not improve his temper, and Pitkin made life a burden to old Gabe and the two black stable hands. Gabe swallowed the abuse with a patient smile, but the two roustabouts muttered to themselves and eyed their employer with malevolence. They had also been missing pay days.

One evening Pitkin stuck his head out of the door of the tackle-room and called for his trainer.

"Gabe! Oh, Gabe! Now where is that good-for-nothing old nigger?"

"Comin', suh, comin'," answered Gabe, shuffling along the line of stalls. "Yo' want to see me, boss?"

"Shut the door behind you," growled Pitkin. "I was thinking it was about time we cut this Sergeant Smith colt loose."

"Yes, suh," answered Gabe. "He's ready to go, boss."

"How good is he?" demanded Pitkin.

"Well, suh," replied Gabe, "he's a heap better'n whut he's been showin' lately, that's a fact."

"Can he beat horses like Calloway and Hartshorn?"

"He kin if he gits a chance."

"How do you mean, a chance?"

"Well, suh, if he gits a good, hones' ride, fo' one thing. He been messed all oveh the race track las' few times out."

"But with a good ride you think he can win?"

"Humph!" sniffed Gabe. "He leave 'em like they standin' still!"

"I want to slip him into the fourth race next Saturday," said Pitkin, "and he'll have Calloway and Hartshorn to beat. There ought to be a nice price on him—4 or 5 to 1, anyway, on account of what he's been showing lately."

"Yo' goin' bet on him, suh?"

"Straight and place," said Pitkin, "but I won't bet a nickel here at the track. They'll be asking you about the colt and trying to get a line on him. You tell 'em that I'm starting him a little bit out of his class just to see if he's game—any lie will do. And if they ask you about the stable money, we're not playing him this time."

"Yes, suh."

"You're absolutely sure he's ready?"

"Ready? Why, boss, ain't yo' been watchin' the way that colt is workin'? Yo' kin bet 'em till they quits takin' it an' not be scared."

"That's all I want to know, Gabe, and mind what I told you about keeping that big mouth of yours shut. If I hear of any talk——"

"I ain't neveh talked yit, has I?"

"Well, don't pick this time to start; that's all."

That night the lights burned late in two tackle-rooms. In one of them Old Man Curry was bringing the judgment of Solomon down to date and fitting it to turf conditions; in the other Henry M. Pitkin was preparing code telegrams to certain business associates in Seattle, Portland, Butte, and San Francisco, for this was in the unregenerate days when pool rooms operated more or less openly in the West. Mr. Pitkin was getting ready for the annual clean-up.

The next morning he was on hand early enough to see General Duval return from an exercise gallop, and there was a small black boy on the colt's back.

"Come here, Gabe," said Pitkin. "Ain't that Curry's nigger jockey?"

"Yes, suh; that's Jockey Moseby Jones, suh."

"What's he doing around this stable?"

"He kind o' gittin' acquainted with the Gen'al, suh."

"Acquainted? What for?"

"Well, suh, they's a maiden race nex' Satu'day, an' I was thinkin' mebbe the Gen'al could win it if he gits a good ride. Jockey Jones didn't have no otheh engagement, suh, so I done hired him fo' the 'casion."

"Oh, you did, did you? Now listen to me, Gabe: I don't want anybody from the Curry stable hanging around this place. Chances are this little nigger will be trying to pick up an earful to carry back to his boss, the psalm-singing old hypocrite! If Curry should find out we're leveling with Sergeant Smith next Saturday, he might go into the ring and hurt the price. I can't stop you putting the little nigger on your own horse, but if he tries to make my barn a hangout, I'll warm his jacket for him, understand? You can tell him so."

"Yes, suh," answered Gabe meekly. "Mist' Curry an' yo' bad friends, boss?"

"We ain't any kind of friends," snapped Pitkin, "and that goes for every blackbird that eats out of his hand!"

"I thought he was a kin' o' pious ole gentleman," said Gabe.

"He's got a lot of people fooled, Curry has," replied Pitkin with unnecessary profanity, "but I've had his number right along. He's a crook, but he gets away with it on account of that long-tailed coat—the sanctimonious old scoundrel! Don't you have anything to do with him, Gabe."

"*Me?*" said Gabe professing mild astonishment. "Humph! I reckon *not!*"

"Always stick with your friends," said Pitkin, "and remember which side your bread is buttered on."

"That's whut I'm aimin' to do, suh. Yo' know, boss, I sort o' figgeh the Gen'al's got a mighty good chance nex' Satu'day in that secon' race. A mighty good chance."

Pitkin sneered. "Going to bet on him, are you?"

"No, suh; not 'less some people pay me whut they owes me."

"You'd only blow it in if you had it," replied Pitkin. "The General's a darn bad race horse—always was and always will be."

"They ain't nothin' in that race fo' him to beat," responded Gabe.

"He's never had anything to beat yet," said Pitkin, "and he's still a maiden, ain't he? Better let him run for the purse, Gabe. Playing a horse like that is just throwing good money after bad."

"Mebbe yo' right, boss," answered the old negro. "Mebbe yo' right, but I still thinks he's got a chance."

Now, in a maiden race every horse is supposed to have a chance, not a particularly robust one, of course, but still a chance. The maidens are the horses which have never won a race, and every jungle circuit is well supplied with these equine misfits. They graduate, one at a time, from their lowly state, and the owner is indeed fortunate who wins enough to cover the cost of probation. The betting on a maiden race is seldom heavy, but always sporadic enough to prove the truth of the old saw about the hope which springs eternal.

Saturday's maiden race was no exception. There was a sizzling paddock tip on The Cricket, a nervous brown mare which had twice finished second at the meeting, the last time missing her graduation by a nose; others had heard that Athelstan was "trying"; there was a rumour that Laredo was about to annex his first brackets; suspicion pointed to Miller Boy as likely to "do something," but nobody had heard any good news of General Duval. Those who looked him up in the form charts found his previous races sufficiently disgraceful.

The Cricket opened favourite at 8 to 5, and when her owner heard this he grunted deep and soulfully and swore by all his gods that the price was too short and the mare a false favourite. He had hoped for not less than 4 to 1, in which case he would have sent the mare out to win, carrying a few hundred dollars of ill-gotten gains as wagers, but at 8 to 5 tickets on The Cricket had no value save as souvenirs of a sad occasion.

Nobody bothered about General Duval; nobody questioned old Gabe as he led a blanketed horse round and round the paddock stalls. Old Man Curry sat on the fence, thoughtfully chewing fine-cut tobacco and seemingly taking no interest in his surroundings, but he saw Pitkin as soon as that fox-faced gentleman entered the paddock, and thereafter he watched the disciple of the double-cross closely. It was plain that Pitkin's visit had no business significance; he was not the sort of man to play a maiden race, and after a few bantering remarks addressed to old Gabe he drifted back into the betting ring, where he made a casual note of the fact that on most of the slates General Duval was quoted at 40 to 1.

"Anybody betting on the nigger's skate?" asked Pitkin of a black man whom he knew.

"Not a soul," was the reply. "What does the old fool start him for?"

"Because that's what he is—an old fool," answered Pitkin briefly as he moved away.

When the first bookmaker chalked up 50 to 1 on the General, a bulky, flat-footed negro, dressed in a screaming plaid suit with an ancient straw hat tilted sportively over one eye, fished a wrinkled two-dollar bill out of his vest pocket, and bet it on Gabriel Johnson's horse. "You like that one, do you?" grinned the bookmaker.

"No, suh, not 'specially," chuckled the negro, "but I sutny likes that long price!"

Soon there was more 50 to 1 in sight, and the flat-footed negro began to shuffle about the betting-ring, bringing to light other wrinkled two-dollar bills. The bookmakers were glad to take in a few dollars on General Duval, if for no other reason than to round out their sheets. The flat-footed negro continued to bet until he arrived at the bottom of his vest pocket, and then he began to draw upon a fund concealed in the fob pocket of his trousers. When the first bugle call sounded he was betting from the right hip—and never more than two dollars at a time.

Jockey Moseby Jones, gorgeous as a tropical butterfly in the cherry jacket with green sleeves and the red, white and blue cap, pranced into General Duval's paddock stall and listened intently as old Gabe bent over him.

"Yo' ain't fo'got whut we tole yo' last night, son?" asked Gabe in anxious tones.

"Ain't fo'got nuthin'," was the sober answer.

"'Cause eve'ything 'pend on how it *look*."

"Uh huh," replied little Mose. "I make it *look* all right."

"This hoss, he might take a notion to run off an' leave 'em soon as the barrier go up," cautioned Gabe. "Keep him folded up in yo' lap to the las' minute."

"An' then set him down," supplemented Mose. "Yo' jus' be watchin' me, thass all!"

"Lot of folks'll be watchin' yo'," warned Gabe. "Them judges, they goin' be watchin' yo'. Remembeh, it got to look *right*!"

As Jockey Jones passed out of the paddock he clucked to his mount and glanced over toward the fence where Old Man Curry was still sitting.

"Hawss," whispered little Mose, "did yo' see that? The ole man winked at us!"

There must have been some truth in the rumour concerning Laredo, for he rushed to the front when the barrier rose, with Miller Boy and Athelstan in hot pursuit. As for The Cricket, she was all but left at the post, and her owner remarked to himself that he'd teach 'em when to make *his* mare a false favourite.

The three people most interested in the cherry jacket with the green sleeves watched it go bobbing along the rail several lengths behind the leaders, and were relieved to find it there instead of out in front. Had the judges been watching the bay colt they could not have helped noticing that his mouth was wide open, due to a powerful pull on the reins, and they might have drawn certain conclusions from this, but they were watching The Cricket instead and mentally putting a rod in pickle for the owner of the favourite.

Laredo led around the turn and into the stretch with Miller Boy and Athelstan crowding him hard, but the pace was beginning to tell on the front runners, and the rear guard was closing in on them, headed by the cherry jacket.

"It's anybody's race," remarked the presiding judge as he squinted up the stretch. "Lord, what a lot of beetles!"

"Yes, they're rotten," said the associate judge. "Laredo's quitting already. Now, then, you hounds, come on! Whose turn is it to-day?"

The maidens came floundering down to the wire spread out like a cavalry charge and covering half the track. At the sixteenth pole a bold man would have hesitated to pick the winner; indeed, it looked to be anybody's race, with the sole exception of The Cricket, sulking far in the rear. It was Gabe Johnson who saw that the wraps were still about Mose's wrists, but it was Old Man Curry who chuckled to himself as the horses passed the paddock gate, and it was Shanghai, Curry's negro hostler, who began to count tickets on General Duval.

"The old nigger's horse is going to be there or thereabouts to-day," commented the presiding judge. "Just—about—there—or—thereabouts. Keep your eye on him, Ed—there he is on the inside. Darn these spread-eagle finishes! They always look bad from angle!"

Thirty yards away from home a single length separated the first five horses, and the fifth horse carried the racing colours of Gabriel Johnson. It was cutting it fine, very fine, but little Mose had an excellent eye for distance; he felt the strength of the mount under him and timed his closing rush to the fraction of a second. Those who were yelling wildly for Athelstan, Miller Boy, and the others saw a flash of cherry jacket on the rail, caught a glimpse of a bullet-headed little negro hurling himself forward in the stirrups—and the race was over. Jockey Moseby Jones had brought a despised outsider home a winner by half a length. There was a stunned silence as the numbers dropped into place, broken only by one terrific whoop from Shanghai, betting commissioner.

"Well," said the associate judge, looking at his chief, "what do you make of that? The winner had a lot left, didn't he? Think the old nigger has been cheating with him?"

The presiding judge rubbed his chin.

"No-o, Ed, I reckon not," said he. "It was a poor race, run in slow time. And we've got to figure that the change of jockeys would make a difference; this Jones is a better boy than Duval is used to. I reckon it's all right—and I'm glad the old nigger finally won a race."

"The Cricket would have walked home if she'd got away good," said the associate judge.

"Have to look into that business," said the other. "Well, I'm glad the old darky finally put one over!"

Many people seemed glad of it, even Mr. Pitkin, who slapped Gabe on the back as he led the winner from the ring.

"Didn't see the race—I was down getting another drink—but they tell me the General just lucked in on the last jump. Everything dead in front of him, eh?"

"Yes, suh," answered Gabe, passing the halter to one of the black stable hands. "It did look like he win lucky, that's a fac'!"

"Well, don't go to celebrating and overlook that fourth race!" ordered Pitkin. "No gin now! You bring Sergeant Smith over to the paddock yourself."

"Yes, suh, boss."

"And if anybody asks you about him, he's only in there for a tryout."

"Jus' fo' a tryout, yes, suh."

To such as were simple enough to expect a crooked man to return straight answers to foolish questions, Pitkin stated (1) that he was not betting a plugged nickel on his colt, (2) that he hardly figured to have a chance with such horses as Calloway and Hartshorn, (3) that he might possibly be third if he got the best of the breaks, and (4) that he had lost his regular jockey and was forced to give the mount to a bad little boy about whom he knew nothing.

The real truth he uncovered to Jockey Shea, a freckled young savage who had taken up the burden where Mulligan laid it down.

"Listen, kid, and don't make any mistakes with this colt. I'm down on him hook, line, and sinker to win and place, so give him a nice ride and I'll declare you in with a piece of the dough. Eh? Never you mind; it'll be *enough*. Now, then, this is a mile race, and Calloway will go out in front—he always does. Lay in behind him and stay there till you get to the head of the stretch, then shake up the colt and come on with him. He can stand a long, hard drive under whip and spur, so give it to him good and plenty from the quarter pole home. Don't try to draw a close finish—win just as far as you can with him, because Hartshorn will be coming from behind."

This was the race as programmed; this was the Pitkin annual clean-up as planned. Imagine, then, Pitkin's sheer, dumb amazement at the spectacle of Shea, going to the bat at the rise of the barrier in order to keep his mount within striking distance of the tail end of the procession! Imagine his wrath as the colt continued to lag in last place, losing ground in spite of the savage punishment administered by Shea. Imagine his sensations when he thought of the Pitkin bank roll, scattered in all the pool rooms between Seattle and San Francisco, tossed to the winds, burned up, gone forever, bet on a colt that would not or could not make a respectable fight for it!

Let us drop the curtain over the rest of the race—Hartshorn won it in a neck-and-neck drive with Calloway just as Shea was flogging the bay colt past the sixteenth pole—and we will lift the curtain again at the point where the judges summoned Pitkin into the stand to ask him for an explanation of Sergeant Smith's pitiful showing.

"Now, sir," said the presiding judge; "we've been pretty lenient with you, Mr. Pitkin. We've overlooked a lot of things that we didn't like—a lot of things. I figured this colt to have a fair chance to win to-day, or be in the money at least. He ran like a cow. How do you account for that?"

"Why, judges," stammered Pitkin, "I—I don't account for it. I *can't* account for it. The colt's been working good, and—and——"

"And you thought he had a chance, did you?"

"Why sure, judges, and I——"

"Well, then, why did you tell your friends that the colt was only in for a tryout? How about that?"

"I—I didn't want 'em spoiling the price, I mean, judges; I didn't think it was anybody's business."

"Oh, so you bet on him, did you? Let's see the tickets."

And of course Mr. Pitkin had no tickets to show. He offered to produce copies of telegrams, but the judges had him exactly where they had been wanting to get him and they gave him a very unhappy ten minutes. At the end of this period the presiding judge cleared his throat and pronounced sentence. "Your entries are refused from now on, and you are warned off this track. Take your horses somewhere else, sir, and don't ever bring 'em back here. That's all."

To Pitkin it seemed enough.

He walked down the steps in a daze and wandered away in the general direction of his stable. He was still in a daze when he reached his destination, and the first thing he saw was old Gabe, his coat on and a satchel in his hand.

"Oh, you've heard about it already, have you?" asked Pitkin dully.

"Heard whut?" And Gabe did not touch the brim of his hat.

"We've got the gate—been warned off: entries refused."

"Glory!" ejaculated the aged trainer. "Time they was gittin' onto you!"

"What's that?" shouted Pitkin. "Why, you black hound, I'll——"

"Yo' won't do nuthin'!" said Gabe stoutly. "Pitkin, yo' an' me is *through*; yo' an' me is *done*! Yo' made me all the trouble yo' eveh goin' make. Nex' time they ketches yo' cheatin' on a race track I hopes they shoot yo' head off!"

Old Gabe walked away toward the Curry barn, and all Pitkin could do was stare after him. Then he sat down on a bale of hay and took stock of his misfortunes.

"I reckon everything's all right, Gabe," said Old Man Curry, who was counting money in his tackle-room. "It was sort o' risky. When a man can't tell his own hoss when he sees him, anything is liable to happen to him on a bush track. I've just cut this bank roll in two, Gabe, and here's your bit. Shanghai's a good bettin' commissioner, eh?"

Old Gabe's eyes bulged as he contemplated the size of his fortune.

"All this, suh—mine?"

"All yours—an' you better not miss that six o'clock train. Never can tell what'll happen, you know, Gabe. Pitkin will keep General Duval, I reckon?"

Gabe grinned from ear to ear.

"I fo'got to tell him so," he chuckled, "but he got both them hosses now. Mist' Curry, whut yo' reckon Sol'mun would say 'bout us?"

"'The Lord will not suffer the soul of the righteous to famish,'" quoted the horseman, "'but he casteth away the substance of the wicked.'"

"A-a-men!" said old Gabe. "An' a fine job o' castin' away been done this evenin'! Mist' Curry, I'm quit hoss racin' now, but yo' the whites' man I met in all my time."

"Go 'way with you!" laughed Curry.

It was one of the black stable hands who recalled Pitkin to a sense of his responsibilities. The roustabout approached, leading a bay colt.

"Boss, is Gabe done quit us?"

"Huh?" grunted Pitkin, emerging from a deep-brown study. "Yes, he's gone, confound him!"

"Well, he lef thisyer Gen'al Duval hoss behin' him. The Gen'al's cooled out now; whut you want me to do with him?"

"Put him in his stall," mumbled Pitkin. "To-morrow I'll see if I can get rid of him."

It is a very stupid race horse which does not know its own stall. The stable hand released his hold on the halter and slapped the colt's flank.

"G'long with yo'!" said he.

Then, and not until then, did Henry M. Pitkin begin to estimate his misfortune correctly, for the bay colt which had won the maiden race in the name of General Duval and carried the racing colours of Gabriel Johnson to their first and only victory marched straight into Sergeant Smith's stall and thrust his muzzle into Sergeant Smith's feed box!